Edited by Natasha Tabori Fried
and Lena Tabori

OBAMA

welcome
BOOKS
New York ● San Francisco

CONTENTS

ESSAYS

EXCERPTS

FACTS

LEGENDS & LORE

POETRY

RECIPES

SONGS

THE SLOW PACIFIC SWELL

BY YVOR WINTERS

Far out of sight forever stands the sea,
Bounding the land with pale tranquility.
When a small child, I watched it from a hill
At thirty miles or more. The vision still
Lies in the eye, soft blue and far away:
The rain has washed the dust from April day;
Paint-brush and lupine lie against the ground;
The wind above the hill-top has the sound
Of distant water in unbroken sky;
Dark and precise the little steamers ply—
Firm in direction they seem not to stir.
That is illusion. The artificer
Of quiet, distance holds me in a vise
And holds the ocean steady to my eyes.

Once when I rounded Flattery, the sea
Hove its loose weight like sand to tangle me
Upon the washing deck, to crush the hull;
Subsiding, dragged flesh at the bone. The skull

Felt the retreating wash of dreaming hair.
Half drenched in dissolution, I lay bare.
I scarcely pulled myself erect; I came
Back slowly, slowly knew myself the same.
That was the ocean. From the ship we saw
Gray whales for miles: the long sweep of the jaw,
The blunt head plunging clean above the wave.
And one rose in a tent of sea and gave
A darkening shudder; water fell away;
The whale stood shining, and then sank in spray.

A landsman, I. The sea is but a sound.
I would be near it on a sandy mound,

And hear the steady rushing of the deep
While I lay stinging in the sand with sleep.
I have lived inland long. The land is numb.
It stands beneath the feet, and one may come
Walking securely, till the sea extends
Its limber margin, and precision ends.
By night a chaos of commingling power,
The whole Pacific hovers hour by hour.
The slow Pacific swell stirs on the sand,
Sleeping to sink away, withdrawing land,
Heaving and wrinkled in the moon, and blind;
Or gathers seaward, ebbing out of mind.

When I am in California, I am not in the west, I am west of the west.

—President Theodore Roosevelt

Well, East coast girls are hip.
I really dig those styles they wear;
And the Southern girls with the way they talk,
They knock me out when I'm down there.

The midwest farmer's daughters really make you feel alright,
And Northern girls with the way they kiss
They keep their boyfriends warm at night.

Chorus
I wish they all could be California,
I wish they all could be California,
I wish they all could be California Girls.

West coast has the sunshine,
and the girls all get so tanned;
I dig a French bikini on Hawaiian Islands,
Dolls by a palm tree in the sand.

I been all around this great big world and I've seen all kinds of girls,
But I couldn't wait to get back in the states,
Back to the cutest girls in the world.

Chorus

CALIFORNIA
GIRLS

BY BRIAN WILSON

BIZARRE & INTERESTING
BUT TRUE

※ ※ ※

The some 200 bison still roaming Catalina Island's hinterlands off the California coast are descendents of a few brought there in the 1920s for a movie.

※ ※ ※

The drawbridge to Sleeping Beauty's 77-foot-tall castle in Disneyland actually works. It was lowered on the park's opening day, July 17, 1955, and has been raised only once since, for renovations.

※ ※ ※

The very first product produced by Hewlett-Packard—Silicon Valley's very first tech company—was an audio oscillator bought by Walt Disney Studios in 1938 for use in the making of *Fantasia*.

※ ※ ※

Thousands make the pilgrimage every year to Hollywood's Westwood Memorial Cemetery to pay respects at Marilyn Monroe's crypt.

※ ※ ※

Across town at Hollywood Memorial Park, visitors can view the grave of Mel Blanc, "The Man of 1,000 Voices" (including Bugs Bunny and Porky Pig), whose headstone reads "That's all, folks!"

※ ※ ※

The television show *Seinfeld* was set in New York City; however, the building exterior used for Jerry's apartment house is actually in Los Angeles.

※ ※ ※

Northern California's Altamont Pass contains the world's largest concentration of wind turbines. The 6000 turbines generate 1-1.2 million kilowatts per year. However, due to its unique location on a major bird-migratory route, it also kills more birds of prey than any other wind facility in North America: as many as 1300 a year.

※ ※ ※

There is an organization in Berkeley whose members gather monthly to discuss and honor the garlic plant. Called "The Lovers of the Stinky

Rose," this unusual organization holds an annual garlic festival and publishes a newsletter known as "Garlic Time."

⌘ ⌘ ⌘

In 1928, William Dreyer and Joseph Edy opened a small ice cream store at 3315 Grand Avenue in Oakland, CA, and "Grand" has been part of Dreyer's Grand Ice Cream's name ever since.

⌘ ⌘ ⌘

The packaged salad industry began in 1989 at Fresh Express in Salinas, CA. The family-owned company introduced an iceberg salad in a patented "Keep-

Crisp" bag—designed to regulate oxygen and keep lettuce fresh for up to two weeks without preservatives.

⌘ ⌘ ⌘

When California's first drive-thru hamburger stand was opened by Harry Snyder in 1948 in Baldwin, In-N-Out Burger was born. Today the company has 148 locations in three states.

⌘ ⌘ ⌘

California is the second-largest cheese-making state after Wisconsin—and leads the nation in the production of Hispanic-style cheeses such as Monterey Jack.

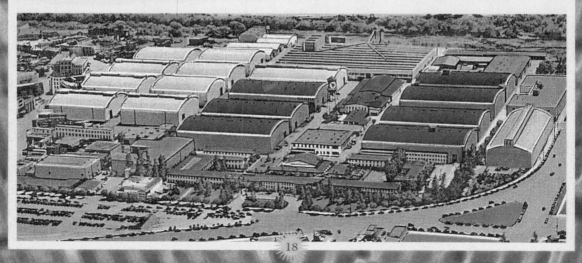

Los Angeles has the dubious distinction of being #1 in the nation for the worst air pollution.

❋ ❋ ❋

Scientists have determined that Los Angeles is moving east, at a rate of about one-fifth of an inch per year.

❋ ❋ ❋

Los Angeles is on the western coast of the United States, but if you were to drive from there to Reno, Nevada, you'd find yourself—strangely enough—headed north*west* (check the map!).

❋ ❋ ❋

Monarch butterflies, migrating to Pacific Grove, California, for better than a century, have given the city the nickname "Butterfly Town, USA."

❋ ❋ ❋

The Directors Guild of America initiated a strike at 6 A.M. on July 14, 1987, against Warner Brothers and Columbia Pictures. Just five minutes later, an agreement was reached. It was the shortest strike in Hollywood history.

❋ ❋ ❋

LSD was legal in California until 1967.

America may be a nation of laws, but California has some real doozies:

In Arcadia, peacocks have right of way.

In Baldwin Park, riding a bike in a swimming pool is illegal.

In Berkeley, you can't whistle for a lost canary before 7 A.M.

In Blythe, you have to own 2 cows in order to wear cowboy boots.

In Chico, there's a $500 fine for detonating a nuclear device within city limits.

In Hollywood, it's illegal to drive more than 2000 sheep down Hollywood Blvd. at once.

In Prunedale, you can't install two bathtubs in one house.

In Redlands, you can't drive on the street unless a man with a lantern walks ahead of you.

In San Diego it's a $250 fine if you leave your Christmas lights up past February 2nd.

A STATE IS BORN

IN 1542, Juan Rodriguez Cabrillo explored the San Diego Bay and claimed the land now known as California for Spain. The area remained largely uncolonized until 1769, when the Spaniards, fearing advancing foreign settlements, decided to establish more-permanent residence and set up a series of missions, presidios (forts), and pueblos (towns).

The 21 missions were established to convert Native Americans to Catholicism and provide Spain with the citizens, labor, and back-up military needed to protect and sustain their regional interests. Over 100 presidios were built to defend the missions and pueblos from foreign invaders. Inhabited mostly by married soldiers and their families, the military outposts also served as political, social, and economic centers for the region. Only three pueblos were officially established under Spanish rule, and as the Spaniards concentrated on protecting New Mexico, the isolated colonists, known as the Californios, lived prosperous, pastoral lives. Mexico won its independence from Spain in 1821, and in the 1830s, the ruling Mexicans secularized the missions.

Using newly discovered overland routes, American immigrants began arriving to the area in large numbers. The Californios drove out the last Mexican governor in 1845, and in 1848, Mexico formally ceded the region to the United States. The Gold Rush of 1849 brought thousands more Americans to San Francisco and its vicinity. California entered the Union in 1850, and, after a few failed experiments, Sacramento was named the capital.

In 1869, with the help of Chinese laborers, a transcontinental railroad was completed. Though the Chinese were originally welcomed in California, their presence came to be seen as a threat when the state's economy lagged, leading to the Chinese Exclusion Act of 1882 The 1884 railroad-rate war and 1885 real estate boom triggered a new wave of overland immigration, and turn-of-the-century industrialization attracted even more settlers. Los Angeles soon had more inhabitants than San Francisco, which was badly damaged by a 1906 earthquake.

Tensions rose over Japanese immigrant farming and trucking practices, and in 1913, the California Alien Land Act was passed, prohibiting non-U.S. citizens from owning agricultural land in California. Settlers continued to stream in, lured by a 1920s real estate boom and the promise of jobs in the 1930s. During World War II, Japanese immigrants were confined in overcrowded "relocation centers."

But during the war, from 1939 to 1945, Californian ship and aircraft production grew rapidly, attracting evermore workers, many of them African Americans. As the African-American population increased, so did racial tensions. In 1965, riots broke out in Los Angeles, sparking riots across the country. The 1960s also saw migrant-farm workers striking for better wages and conditions and widespread student protesting. During the 1970s and 1980s, California continued its rapid growth, largely because of immigrants from the Philippines, China, and Southeast Asia, as well as heavy illegal Mexican immigration. As cuts in federal defense spending and the increased population strained California's economy, social pressures again mounted. In 1992, more riots swept through Los Angeles, killing 55 people, injuring approximately 2,000, and causing over $13 billion in damages.

By late 2000, due to 1990s deregulation of the electricity industry, California faced rolling blackouts and large electricity rate hikes. Because of the ensuing economic slump and state budget shortfalls, Governor Gray Davis was recalled and actor Arnold Schwarzenegger was elected to replace him. California is currently the most populated state in the United States, leading the nation in fruits, vegetables, and dairy production. In addition, California boasts much of the United States' domestic wine and motion picture/entertainment production, as well as a heavy concentration of information technology developers and a flourishing tourism industry.

ZIP!

Huevos Rancheros

Huevos Rancheros, or "rancher's eggs," is an extremely popular dish in Mexico where eggs are eaten for most any meal. Our neighbors to the south brought their spicy egg dishes to California where they are enjoyed burrito style, with salsas, or accompanied by beans and rice. Our recipe also includes another California favorite, avocado, which perfectly offsets the spicy salsa.

1. Heat oil in a small skillet over medium-high heat. Fry tortillas one at a time until firm, but not crisp. Place on paper towels to drain any excess grease.

2. Meanwhile, combine the refried beans and 1 tablespoon of butter in a small saucepan or microwave-safe dish. Cover, and cook until heated through.

3. Heat remaining butter in a skillet and fry eggs to desired consistency.

4. Place fried tortillas onto serving plates. Spread a layer of beans on them. Top with a fried egg, cheese, crumbled bacon, salsa, and sliced avocado.

5. If you prefer your cheese a bit more melted, place under a broiler on high for 45 seconds to 1 minute, or until cheese is hot and bubbling. Serve.

Serves 4

2 tablespoons vegetable oil

4 6-inch corn tortillas

1 cup refried beans with green chilies

2 tablespoon butter

4 eggs

1 cup shredded sharp cheddar cheese

8 slices bacon, cooked and crumbled

1 cup salsa

1 avocado, sliced

FROM EAST OF EDEN

BY JOHN STEINBECK

The Salinas Valley is in Northern California. It is a long narrow swale between two ranges of mountains, and the Salinas River winds and twists up the center until it falls at last into Monterey Bay.

I remember my childhood names for grasses and secret flowers. I remember where a toad may live and what time the birds awaken in the summer—and what trees and seasons smelled like—how people looked and walked and smelled even. The memory of odors is very rich.

I remember that the Gabilan Mountains to the east of the valley were light gay mountains full of sun and loveliness and a kind of invitation, so that you wanted to climb into their warm foothills, almost as you want to climb into the lap of a beloved mother. They were beckoning mountains with a brown grass love. The Santa Lucias stood up against the sky to the west and kept the valley from the open sea, and they were dark and brooding—unfriendly and dangerous. I always found in myself a dread of west and a love of east. Where I ever got such an idea I cannot say, unless it could be that the morning came over the peaks of the Gabilans and the night drifted back from the ridges of the Santa Lucias. It may be that the birth and death of the day had some part in my feeling about the two ranges of mountains.

From both sides of the valley little streams slipped out of the hill canyons and fell into the bed of the Salinas River. In the winter of wet years the streams ran full-freshet, and they swelled the river until sometimes it raged and boiled, bank full, and then it was a destroyer. The river tore the edges of the farm lands and washed whole acres down; it toppled barns and houses into itself, to go floating and bobbing away. It trapped cows and pigs and sheep and drowned them in its muddy brown water and carried them to the sea. Then when the late spring came, the river drew in from its edges and the sand banks appeared. And in the summer the river didn't run at all above ground. Some pools would be left in the deep swirl places under a high bank. The rules and grasses grew back, and willows straightened up with the flood debris in their upper branches. The Salinas was only a part-time river. The summer sun drove it underground. It was not a fine river at all, but it was the only one we had and so we boasted about it—how dangerous it was in a wet winter and how dry it was in a dry summer. You can boast about anything if it's all you have. Maybe the less you have, the more you are required to boast.

The floor of the Salinas Valley, between the ranges and below the foothills, is level because this valley used to be the bottom of a hundred-miles inlet from the sea. The river mouth at Moss Landing was centuries ago the entrance to this long inland water. Once, fifty miles down the valley, my father bored a well. The drill came up first with topsoil and then with gravel and then with white sea sand full of shells and even pieces of whalebone. There were twenty feet of sand and then black earth again, and even a piece of redwood, that imperishable wood that does not rot. Before the inland sea the valley must have been a forest. And those things had happened right under our feet. And it seemed to me sometimes at night that I could feel both the sea and the redwood forest before it.

On the wide level acres of the valley the topsoil lay deep and fertile. It required only a rich winter of rain to make it break forth in grass and flowers. The spring flowers in a wet year were unbelievable. The whole valley floor, and the foothills too, would be carpeted with lupins and poppies. Once a woman told me that colored flowers would seem more bright if you added a few white flowers to give the colors definition. Every petal of blue lupin is edged with white, so that a field of lupins is more blue than you can imagine. And mixed with these were splashes of California poppies. These too are of a burning color—not orange, not gold, but if pure gold were liquid and could raise a cream, that golden cream might be like the color of the poppies. When their season was over the yellow mustard came up and grew to a great height. When my grandfather came into the valley the mustard was so tall that a man on horseback showed only his head above the yellow flowers. On the uplands the grass would be strewn with buttercups, with hen-and-chickens, with black centered yellow violets. And a little later in the season there would be red and yellow stands of Indian paintbrush. These were the flowers of the open places exposed to the sun.

Under the live oaks, shaded and dusky, the maidenhair flourished and gave a good smell, and under the mossy banks of the water courses whole clumps of five-fingered ferns and goldy-backs hung down. Then there were harebells, tiny lanterns, cream white and almost sinful looking, and these were so rare and magical that a child, finding one, felt singled out and special all day long.

When June came the grasses headed out and turned brown, and the hills turned a brown which was not brown but a gold and saffron and red—an indescribable color. And from then on until the next rains the earth dried and the streams stopped. Cracks appeared on the level ground. The Salinas River sank under its sand. The wind blew down the valley, picking up dust and straws, and grew stronger and harsher as it went south. It stopped in the evening. It was a rasping nervous wind, and the dust particles cut into a man's skin and burned his eyes. Men working in the fields wore goggles and tied handkerchiefs around their noses to keep the dirt out.

The valley land was deep and rich, but the foothills wore only a skin of topsoil no deeper than the grass roots; and the farther up the hills you went, the thinner grew the soil, with flints sticking through, until at the brush line it was a kind of dry flinty gravel that reflected the hot sun blindingly.

I had spoken of the rich years when the rainfall was plentiful. But there were dry years too, and they put a terror on the valley. The water came in a thirty-year cycle. There would be five or six wet and wonderful years when there might be nineteen to twenty-five inches of rain, and the land would shout with grass. Then would come six or seven pretty good years of twelve to sixteen inches of rain. And then the dry years would come, and sometimes there would be only seven or eight inches of rain. The land dried up and the grasses headed out miserably a few inches high and great bare scabby places appeared in the valley. The live oaks got a crusty look and the sagebrush was gray. The land cracked and the springs dried up and the cattle listlessly nibbled dry twigs. Then the farmers and the ranchers would be filled with disgust for the Salinas Valley. The cows would grow thin and sometimes starve to death. People would have to haul water in barrels to their farms just for drinking. Some families would sell out for nearly nothing and move away. And it never failed that during the dry years the people forgot about the rich years, and during the wet years they lost all memory of the dry years. It was always that way.

It used to be said that you had to know what was happening in America because it gave us a glimpse of our future. Today, the rest of America, and after that Europe, had better heed what happens in California, for it already reveals the type of civilization that is in store for all of us.

—Alistair Cooke

MOMENTS IN HISTORY

❀ ❀ ❀

Native California Indians and Europeans first met in 1533, when the Spaniards who had conquered the Aztecs traveled northward and encountered the Guayacura tribe at the Bay of La Paz in Baja, California.

❀ ❀ ❀

On November 29, 1777, the first civilian town (or pueblo), San Jose, was established to help supply the military presidios of San Francisco and Monterey.

❀ ❀ ❀

The first wagon train of American settlers from the East arrived in California in 1841.

❀ ❀ ❀

On October 24, 1861, the first telegraph was sent from California commemorating the completion of the first transcontinental telegraph line. It rendered the Pony Express obsolete.

❀ ❀ ❀

By 1870 disease, malnutrition, and a campaign of extermination carried out by white settlers reduced the number of Native Americans in California from 150,000 to 30,000.

❀ ❀ ❀

As a result of a rate war among the railroads, in 1887, fares dropped from $125 to as low as a $1 for a trip to California. More than 200,000 people moved to southern California that year alone.

❀ ❀ ❀

John Muir founded the Sierra Club in 1892, dedicated to "preserving the forests and other natural features of the Sierra Nevada."

❀ ❀ ❀

The California State Automobile Association was founded in 1901. It is the oldest auto club in America.

❅ ❅ ❅

California became the sixth state in the Union to grant women's suffrage in 1911.

❅ ❅ ❅

Los Angeles hosted the Xth Olympiad in 1932, in the midst of the Great Depression.

❅ ❅ ❅

The Pan-Pacific International Exposition of 1915 celebrated the completion of the Panama Canal as well as the rebuilding of San Francisco after the 1906 earthquake and fire. The only exhibit that remains now is the Palace of Fine Arts, which houses the Exploratorium Museum.

❅ ❅ ❅

Hoover Dam was dedicated by President Franklin Delano Roosevelt on September 11, 1936. The dam, which is the size of a 60-story building, holds back the largest reservoir in the world, Lake Mead, in order to divert water from the Colorado River to southern California.

❅ ❅ ❅

John Steinbeck won the Pulitzer Prize for his novel *The Grapes of Wrath*, in 1940. The story of the evolution of an Oklahoma family from farmers to migrant workers as they make their way to California hit home with a nation recovering from the Great Depression.

❅ ❅ ❅

California became the most populous state in 1964, surpassing New York.

❅ ❅ ❅

Californians elected popular former-actor Ronald Reagan as their governor in 1966. He went to become President of the United States in 1980.

❅ ❅ ❅

Lawrence Ferlinghetti became San Francisco's first Poet Laureate in 1998. He founded City Lights Booksellers and Publishers in 1953, which then became a lightning rod for a new generation of untamed poets in 1956 with its publication of Allen Ginsberg's "Howl."

ON A PLANET OF LIMITED AREA, the more people there are, the less vacant space there is bound to be. Over and above the material and sociological problems of increasing population, there is a serious psychological problem. In a completely homemade environment, such as is provided by any great metropolis, it is as hard to remain sane as it is in a completely natural environment such as the

TOMORROW AND TOMORROW AND TOMORROW

BY ALDOUS HUXLEY

desert or the forest. O Solitude, where are thy charms? But O Multitude, where are *thine*? The most wonderful thing about America is that, even in these middle years of the twentieth century, there are so few Americans. By taking a certain amount of trouble you might still be able to get yourself eaten

by a bear in the state of New York. And without any trouble at all you can get bitten by a rattler in the Hollywood hills, or die of thirst, while wandering through an uninhabited desert, within a hundred and fifty miles of Los Angeles. A short generation ago you might have wandered and died within only a hundred miles of Los Angeles. Today the mounting tide of humanity has oozed through the intervening canyons and spilled out into the wide Mojave. Solitude is receding at the rate of four and a half kilometers per annum.

And yet, in spite of it all, the silence persists. For this silence of the desert is such that casual sounds, and even the systematic noise of civilization, cannot abolish it. They coexist with it—as small irrelevances at right angles to an enormous meaning, as veins of something analogous to darkness with an enduring transparency. From the irrigated land come the dark gross sounds of lowing cattle, and above them the plovers trail their vanishing threads of shrillness. Suddenly, startlingly, out of the sleeping sagebrush there burst the shrieking of coyotes—Trio for Ghoul and Two Damned Souls. On the trunks of cottonwood trees, on the wooden walls of barns and houses, the woodpeckers rattle away like pneumatic drills. Picking one's way between the cactuses and the creosote bushes one hears, like some tiny whirring clockwork, the soliloquies of invisible wrens, the calling, at dusk, of nightjays and even occasionally the voice of Homo sapiens—six of the species in a parked Chevrolet, listening to the broadcast of a prize fight, or else in pairs necking to the delicious accompaniment of Crosby. But the light forgives, the distances forget, and this great crystal of silence, whose base is as large as Europe and whose height, for all practical purposes, is infinite, can coexist with things of far higher order of discrepancy than canned sentiment or vicarious sport. Jet planes, for example—the stillness is so massive that it can absorb even jet planes. The screaming crash mounts to its intolerable climax and fades again, mounts as another of the monsters rips through the air, and once more diminishes and is gone. But even at the height of the outrage the mind can still remain aware of that which surrounds it, that which preceded and will outlast it.

Unlike a mountain forest or the ocean, rife with depth and secret, the desert's unveiled openness—its grand sweep of red-hot honesty—requires a period of adjustment and patient, contemplative observation. Desolation transforms under light's tutelage. Everyone ought to witness this transition and their own internal adjustment to it at least once. Preferably alone.

—Camille Cusumano

AS LONG AS I LIVE

BY JOHN MUIR

As long as I live
I'll hear waterfalls and birds and winds sing.
I'll interpret the rocks,
Learn the language of the flood, storm,
and the avalanche.
I'll acquaint myself with the glaciers
And wild gardens,
And get as near the heart of the world as I can.

IT ALL BEGAN on January 24, 1848, when John Sutter hired James Marshall to build a sawmill on the American River. That morning, Marshall spied a shiny little nugget. When he flattened the metal between two rocks, it didn't shatter. And when the cook tested it in a pot of lye, they realized they'd found gold.

Though Sutter tried to keep the discovery a secret, stories of gold spread via travelers and letters to the East Coast and Europe. Trading ships carried gold rumors to Mexico, Chile, Hawaii, and China. Most people first thought the stories to be no more than fantastical tales, but in December of 1848, when 220 ounces of gold arrived in Washington D.C., President Polk confirmed the findings to Congress. The Gold Rush was on.

In 1849, adventurers from around the world, most of them greenhorns who had never worked a field or saddled a horse, abandoned their everyday lives and made their way toward what would soon become California. That year at least 32,000 "forty-niners" from the eastern United States, Canada, and Mexico walked six to nine months overland. In 1850, another 44,000 joined them. But their dreams of gold quickly gave way to the realities of exhaustion, cholera, starvation, and deadly Sierra winters. Forty-niners traveling by sea often endured four to eight months of boredom, seasickness, storms, minimal food, tainted water, over-crowding, rampant disease, and even shipwrecks. Still, from April 1849 to January 1850, close to 40,000 gold seekers made their way to San Francisco via the sea.

THE GOLD RUSH

New arrivals found the gold-rush frontier to be a lawless, classless place that lacked the boundaries and restrictions of settled states and nations. Because of thousands of years of erosion and mountain runoff, gold could initially be found lying in riverbeds, ripe for the picking. Never before could an ordinary individual so easily obtain gold and quickly amass a fortune.

Fortunes were made not only by mining gold. Many savvy entrepreneurs profited by catering to the needs of the miners. Sam Brannan is often credited for starting the boom by running through the streets of San Francisco shouting, "Gold in the American River!" and waving a bottle of gold dust. But before Brannan spread the news, he'd bought up every pick, pan, and shovel in the region, eventually selling a 20-cent pan for 15 dollars. In nine weeks, Brannan made 36 thousand dollars. He went on to become the wealthiest man in California, even minting his own money. Other notable businessmen of the era include Levi Strauss, who stitched the sturdy canvas pants the miners wore; Henry Wells and William Fargo, who offered secure banking, transportation, and mail service to miners far from home; and John Studebaker, who invested his own gold spoils in his family's wagon business, eventually going on to make automobiles.

Foreigners from places such as Mexico, Chile, China, Ireland, Germany, France, and Turkey struck it rich, too. But as streams got crowded, discrimination and ethnic tensions rose, and the state passed laws taxing foreign miners. It was challenging for foreigners to get their gold home because thieves often targeted them. The Chinese were known to forge gold into woks and pots and board ships carrying what appeared to be nothing more than greasy, old cooking utensils.

Though women were scarce, those who did venture west could make good money cooking, laundering, and cleaning for the miners. Even slaves were known to have some success in California. When Southerners arrived with slaves to do their work, the miners objected, mostly because they did not want to equate their own work with "slave labor." Miners also resented people back East who profited from someone else's digging. Consequently, California entered the Union as a free state in 1850—further inciting tensions that led to the Civil War. The true casualties of the gold rush were the Native Americans, who had lived in the region for over 10,000 years. When gold seekers surged into the area, they destroyed the local socioeconomic systems. Tribes were annihilated—their numbers decreased from approximately 300,000 to 50,000 members.

By 1852, nearly 275,000 people had converged on California, making San Francisco the most ethnically and culturally diverse city on the planet. From 1848 to 1853, the city grew from 800 to 50,000 people, racking up two murders per day. In 18 months, a plot of land that had cost $16 rocketed to $45,000. And in less than two years the town had been burned down and rebuilt six times, making use of the half-billion dollars that passed through San Francisco in the 1850s.

But the easy gold was soon gone. Fortune seekers toiled away in cold creeks and dank mines, and as luckless months stretched into years, loneliness, bad food, sickness, harsh weather, and the hard work of mining sunk them into despair. More and more miners took to gambling, drinking, and other vices. Crime and hangings became commonplace.

When gold became harder to find, miners first banded together to dam rivers and expose riverbeds. But more muscle was needed, and corporations soon took over. They used heavy machinery to expose underground gold, wreaking havoc on the environment. Huge floating dredges scraped up millions of tons of river gravel; mercury used to extract gold leaked into rivers, disturbing the food chain; and hydraulic drills blasted apart mountainsides and riverbanks, forever changing landscape of northern California. The prevailing attitude of miners was that it was them against nature, and it took over 30 years to ban hydraulic mining and begin to change this attitude of exploitation.

The legacy of the California Gold Rush is a state infused with an adventurous, entrepreneurial, multi-cultural spirit. California has since spawned other "rushes" including the Hollywood motion picture industry, the defense industry, and the computer industry of Silicon Valley.

Chinese Chicken Salad

THIS ASIAN SPIN ON YOUR EVERYDAY SALAD BECAME POPULAR IN CALIFORNIA DURING THE '60S AND '70S AT A TIME WHEN BOTH CHINESE COOKING AND HEALTH-CONSCIOUS EATING WERE VERY MUCH IN VOGUE. VARIOUS PEOPLE LAY CLAIM TO THE ORIGINAL RECIPE. CHEFS MADAME WONG OF WESTWOOD AND MADAME WU OF SANTA MONICA EACH POPULARIZED A DISTINCT VERSION (MADAME WONG'S IS TOPPED WITH RICE STICKS AND GINGER, AND MADAME WU'S WITH ALMONDS, FRIED WONTONS, AND RICE NOODLES); AND WALLACE TOM OF THE NEW MOON CAFÉ ALSO LAID CLAIM TO ITS INVENTION. WHATEVER ITS ORIGINS, THIS ZESTY SALAD REMAINS A POPULAR STAPLE IN CALIFORNIA RESTAURANTS.

1. Combine all salad ingredients.

2. Combine all dressing ingredients.

3. Toss together and serve.

SERVES 4

4 chicken breasts, shredded
(see Cobb Salad, page 134)

2 heads iceberg lettuce

2 carrots, peeled and shredded

2-3 stalks green onion

¹⁄₂ cup slivered almonds, toasted

¹⁄₄ cup cilantro, coarsely chopped

1 tablespoon toasted sesame seeds

DRESSING:

¹⁄₂ cup red wine vinegar

¹⁄₂ cup soy sauce

¹⁄₄ cup hoisin sauce

Salt to taste

1 tablespoon chili-garlic sauce, or to taste

1 tablespoon fresh ginger, minced

¹⁄₂ cup pickled red ginger, minced

¹⁄₂ cup green onions, minced

1 tablespoon honey

¹⁄₂ cup toasted sesame oil

FROM THE JOY LUCK CLUB

BY *AMY TAN*

When I arrived, nobody asked me questions. The authorities looked at my papers and stamped me in. I decided to go first to a San Francisco address given to me by this girl in Peking. The bus put me down on a wide street with cable cars. This was California Street. I walked up this hill and then I saw a tall building. This was Old St. Mary's. Under the church sign, in handwritten Chinese characters, someone had added: "A Chinese Ceremony to save Ghosts from Spiritual Unrest 7 A.M. and 8:30 A.M." I memorized this information in case the authorities asked me where I worshiped my religion. And then I saw another sign across the street. It was painted on the outside of a short building: "Save Today for Tomorrow, at Bank of America." And I thought to myself, This is where American people worship. See, even this I was not so dumb! Today that church is the same size, but where that short bank used to be, now there is a tall building, fifty stories high, where you and your husband-to-be work and look down on everybody.

My daughter laughed when I said this. Her mother can make a good joke.

So I kept walking up this hill. I saw two pagodas, one on each side of the street, as though they were the entrance to a great Buddha temple. But hen I looked carefully, I saw the pagoda was really just a building topped with stacks of tile roofs, no walls, nothing else under its head.

I was surprised how they tried to make everything look like an old imperial city or an emperor's tomb. But if you looked on either side of these pretend-pagodas, you could see the streets became narrow and crowded, dark, and dirty. I thought to myself, Why did they choose only the worst Chinese parts for the inside? Why didn't they build gardens and ponds instead? Oh, here and there was the look of a famous ancient cave or a Chinese opera. But inside it was always the same cheap stuff.

So by the time I found the address the girl in Peking gave me, I knew not to expect too much. The address was a large green building, so noisy, children running up and down the outside stairs and hallways. Inside number 402, I found an old woman who told me right away she had wasted her time waiting for me all week. She quickly wrote down some addresses and gave them to me, keeping her hand out after I took the paper. So I gave her an American dollar and she looked at it and said, "Syaujye"—Miss—"we are in America now. Even a beggar can starve on this dollar." So I gave her another dollar and she said, "Aii, you think it is so easy getting this information?" So I gave her another and she closed her hand and her mouth.

With the addresses this old woman gave me, I found a cheap apartment on Washington Street. It was like all the other places, sitting on top of a little store. And through this three-dollar list, I found a terrible job paying me seventy-five cents an hour. Oh, I tried to get a job as a salesgirl, but you had to know English for that. I tried for another job as a Chinese hostess, but they also wanted me to rub my hands up and down foreign men, and I knew right away this was as bad as fourth-class prostitutes in

China! So I rubbed that address out with black ink. And some of the other jobs required you to have a special relationship. They were jobs held by families from Canton and Toishan and the Four Districts, southern people who had come many years ago to make their fortune and were still holding onto them with the hands of their great-grandchildren.

So my mother was right about my hardships. This job in the cookie factory was one of the worst. Big black machines worked all day and night pouring little pancakes onto moving round griddles. The other women and I sat on high stools, and as the little pancakes went by, we had to grab them off the hot griddle just as they turned golden. We would put a strip of paper in the center, then fold the cookie in half and bend its arms back just as it turned hard. If you grabbed the pancake too soon, you would burn your fingers on the hot, wet dough. But if you grabbed too late, the cookie would harden before you could even complete the first bend. And then you had to throw these mistakes in a barrel, which counted against you because the owner could sell those only as scraps.

After the first day, I suffered ten red fingers. This was not a job for a stupid person. You had to learn fast or your fingers would turn into fried sausages. So the next day only my eyes burned, from never taking them off the pancakes. And the day after that, my arms ached from holding them out ready to catch the pancakes at just the right moment. But by the end of my first week, it became mindless work and I could relax enough to notice who else was working on each side of me. One was an older woman who never smiled and spoke to herself in Cantonese when

she was angry. She talked like a crazy person. On my other side was a woman around my age. Her barrel contained very few mistakes. But I suspected she ate them. She was quite plump.

"Eh, *Syaujye*," She called to me over the loud noise of the machines. I was grateful to hear her voice, to discover we both spoke Mandarin, although her dialect was coarse-sounding. "Did you ever think you would be so powerful you could determine someone else's fortune?" she asked.

I didn't understand what she meant. So she picked up one of the strips of paper and read it aloud, first in English: "Do not fight and air your dirty laundry in public. To the victor go the soils." Then she translated in Chinese: "You shouldn't fight and do your laundry at the same time. If you win, your clothes will get dirty."

I still did not know what she meant. So she picked up another one and read in English: "Money is the root of all evil. Look around you and dig deep." And then in Chinese: "Money is a bad influence. you become restless and rob graves."

"What is this nonsense?" I asked her, putting the strips of paper in my pocket, thinking I should study these classical American sayings.

"They're fortunes," she explained. "American people think Chinese people write these sayings."

"But we never say such things!" I said. "These things don't make sense. These are not fortunes, they are bad instructions."

"No, Miss," she said, laughing, "it is our bad fortune to be here making these and somebody else's bad fortune to pay to get them."

go west
paradise is there
you'll have all that you can eat
of milk & honey over there

you'll be the brightest star
the world has ever seen
sun-baked slender heroine
of film & magazine

go west
paradise is there
you'll have all that you can eat
of milk & honey over there

you'll be the brightest light
the world has ever seen
the dizzy height of a jet-set life
you could never dream

your pale blue eyes
strawberry hair
lips so sweet
skin so fair

your future bright
beyond compare

it's rags to riches
over there

San Andreas Fault
moved its fingers
through the ground
earth divided
plates collided
such an awful sound

San Andreas Fault
moved its fingers
through the ground
terra cotta shattered
and the walls came
tumbling down

o, promised land
o, wicked ground
build a dream
tear it down

o, promised land
what a wicked ground
build a dream
watch it all fall down

SAN ANDREAS FAULT

BY NATALIE MERCHANT

FIRST SPRING IN CALIFORNIA, 1936

BY WILMA ELIZABETH MCDANIEL

The Oakies wrapped their
old dreams in army blankets
and patchwork quilts
and slept away the foggy
winter nights of 1935

From doorways of tents
and hasty shacks
now and then a boxcar
they watched for spring
as they would watch for
the Second Coming of Christ

And saw the Valley change
from skim milk blue
still needing sweaters
to palest green that filled
their eyes with hope

As they waited for odd jobs
the Valley burst forth
with one imperial color
poppies flung their gold
over acres of sand
like all the bankers in California
gone raving mad

Women wept in wonder
and hunted fruit jars to can
the precious flowers
in case next year
did not produce a bumper crop

In every cove along the line of
mountains the fog was being piled
in higher and higher, as though by
some wind that was inaudible to me.
I could trace its progress, one pine-tree
first growing hazy and then disappearing
after another; although sometimes
there was none of this forerunning haze,
but the whole opaque white ocean
gave a start and swallowed a piece
of mountain at a gulp.

—Robert Louis Stevenson

THE PACIFIC COAST HIGHWAY (or the PCH) is hard to pin down. Obviously, it is a highway that winds along the Pacific Coast—but what is it exactly? Some insist the PCH is California State Highway 1 (or, as shown on maps, Route 1), the road that traces the majestic Big Sur coastline. Others assert the PCH is the much longer US Highway 101, affectionately known as The 101. To still others, the PCH is more of a concept—a combination of scenic roads, including both Highway 1 and The 101, that hug the Pacific Coast and

ON THE ROAD: PACIFIC COAST HIGHWAY

stretch from the Mexican border through California, up the rugged coast of Oregon, and on to the temperate rainforests of Washington state's Olympic Peninsula.

In this larger, glorious conception, the Pacific Coast Highway covers over 2000 miles and offers some of the most spectacular shoreline vistas in the world. Along the way, you can experience an extraordinary range of beautiful, historical, and one-of-a-kind attractions such as the famous Butterfly Trees of Pacific Grove, the 1772 Mission San Luis Obispo de Tolosa, and Half Moon Bay's world championship pumpkin weigh-off.

If you jump in your car in the southernmost part of California and head north, you first hit San Diego and Los Angeles and the warm, sun-drenched surfer beaches of La Jolla, Venice, Santa Monica, Malibu, Santa Barbara, and Pismo. Winding northward, you pass through miles of beaches, wildflowers, and vineyards to arrive at San Simeon and the beginning of Big Sur. A highlight of San Simeon is the surreal Hearst castle, a 165 room palatial mansion built by eccentric publishing magnate William Randolph Hearst that overlooks the Pacific. The 127-acre estate is home to a vast collection of Italian, Spanish, and ancient Greek antiques, countless paintings, beautiful terraces, sparkling pools, sumptuous gardens, and the occasional free-roaming zebra.

The landscape changes significantly as you enter Big Sur, a 90-mile strip of shoreline originally dubbed *El Sur Grand* or "The Big South" by Spaniards of Monterey. To your right, thick pine forests cling to steep mountainsides as the land to your left drops off hundreds of feet into the pounding sea. The road twists along cliff tops and through several state parks, offering you breathtaking views of craggy rocks jutting into pristine blue waters, windswept Cyprus trees, playful sea otters, lolling sea lions, and in winter, if you're lucky, migrating gray whales. The dramatic drive also provides many chances to camp, hike, picnic on the beach, and dine in fine seaside restaurants.

At the northern tip of Big Sur, you enter the rolling hills and fertile pastures of Monterey Peninsula. The peninsula features charming Carmel with its more than 70 art galleries, the world-class Pebble Beach golf course, the historic town of Monterey whose Cannery Row now houses the Monterey Bay Aquarium (boasting the world's largest collection of jelly fish); and loopy, happening Santa Cruz—the proud home of University of California, Santa Cruz and its beloved mascot, the Banana Slug.

The Pacific Coast Highway continues northward through foggy San Francisco, over the fabled Golden Gate Bridge, and on to Napa and Sonoma's bountiful wine country. Another day's drive finds you deep in the fabled redwood groves and near the end of PCH's California leg. If you continue up in through the wilds of Oregon, you are rewarded with old lighthouses, working fishing villages, 300-foot sand dunes, and a long, magnificent bridge that spans the mouth of the Columbia and links Oregon to Washington. The Pacific Coast Highway culminates in upstate Washington, circling around the lush Olympic Peninsula.

WE WENT FIRST into the San Joaquin Valley, naturally this was interesting because Alice Toklas's pioneer grandfather had owned all his land there and Fresno and all about was exciting, after all if that is where you were and the names of it are that it is exciting. We tacked back and forward across the valley and we did like all we saw we liked smelling the oranges and the kind of nuts and fruits that had not been there I had never been there before but she had been there and the way they cut the tops of the trees

FROM **EVERYBODY'S AUTOBIOGRAPHY**

BY GERTRUDE STEIN

to make a straight line as if they had been cut with a razor and the fig trees fig trees smell best of all and we went forward and back until we got a little higher and saw the California poppies growing which we had not seen growing wild since we had been in California, they were like they were and it gave me a shock to see them there, it began to be funny and to make me uneasy. Then we went up a little higher and then although it was still wintry we thought that we would go into the Yosemite, we had neither of us ever been there, that I had not been there was not astonishing,

we had tended to go north not south from Oakland when we were children but that Alice Toklas had not been there was more surprising, her cousins who lived then in the San Joaquin Valley used to drive every year into the valley as they called the Yosemite the others were rivers but not valleys, and so we decided to go into the valley, I wanted to see the big trees I had never seen them and anyway we decided we would go into the valley, it was spring but it was a very cold one, there was rain and there was lots of snow yet and again.

We tried one road that led to big trees but it was raining and snowing and the road looked none too good and precipitous besides perhaps not but I felt that and so we went back again and finally got to Merced, there the sun was shining it was muddy but the sun was shining and the town of Merced looked like the kind of California I knew just a little country town and we ate something there and decided to go on. I am always afraid of precipices and I could not believe that in going into the Yosemite there would not be lots of them, they had told us not but naturally I did not believe them they said the road was not dangerous, of course the road is not dangerous roads rarely are but it is what you see when you don't see anything except the sky that gives you that funny feeling and makes what I call precipitous. No matter how wide the road and how large the curve it can be precipitous to me. So at Merced we wanted to go on but I thought I would feel better if somebody else was along and driving, so we asked was there any one, in France of course there would not have been any one but in Merced of course there was there was a boy at school who sooner or later would have to go home and his home was in the valley so he said he did not mind missing school that afternoon if we gave him a dollar and of course we did not mind and although he was very young he could drive anybody any where in America can. A good many can here in France but not so young as in America, in France they can all ride a bicycle any one can do that and go up any hill and never get off everybody has his specialty.

So we were driven into the valley and there was no precipice, how they made the road as it is and going always higher and never at any time in any place to feel as if you were jumping off and never necessary to change your speed it was a wonder. Later they told us perhaps it is so that you could go all the way from California to New York and at no time is there a grade which makes changing speeds necessary, the road is made in such a way and of course there are some precipitous spots but they all said certainly not and after the Yosemite Valley road I was almost ready to believe them.

The roads in America were lovely, they move along alone the big ones the way the railroad tracks

73

used to move with really no connection with the country. Of course in a way that is natural enough as I always like to tell a Frenchman and he listens but he does not believe the railroad did not follow the towns made by the road but it made a road followed by the towns and the country, there were no towns and no roads therefore no country until the railroad came along, and the new big roads in America still make you feel that way, air lines they call some of them and they are they have nothing really to do with the towns and the country. The only thing that worried me not so much in California but still even there is the soft shoulder of the road as they called it, that the cement road had no finish to it as it has in France which keeps it from being a danger, I suppose the roads are too long to make that possible but still it is a pity, the smaller roads are too narrow as they have a soft shoulder, some day they will make them a little wider and finish the edge of them with a little edge to it, then they will be pleasanter for driving certainly in rain and anyway. However we did like driving on the American roads and the boy brought us safely into Yosemite.

It was high there and cold and we arrived a little late but the director of the valley offered to take us to see the big trees and we went. I liked that. The thing that was most exciting about them was that they had no roots did anybody want anything to be more

interesting than that that the oldest and the solidest and the biggest tree that could be grown had no foundation, there it was sitting and the wind did not blow it over it sat so well. It was very exciting. Very beautiful and very exciting.

The attraction and superiority of California are in its days. It has better days, and more of them, than any other country.

—Ralph Waldo Emerson

BECOMING A REDWOOD

By Dana Gioia

Stand in a field long enough, and the sounds
start up again. The crickets, the invisible
toad who claims that change is possible,

And all the other life too small to name.
First one, then another, until innumerable
they merge into the single voice of a summer hill

Yes, it's hard to stand still, hour after hour,
fixed as a fencepost, hearing the steers
snort in the dark pasture, smelling the manure.

And paralyzed by the mystery of how a stone
can bear to be a stone, the pain
the grass endures breaking through the earth's crust.

Unimaginable the redwoods on the far hill,
rooted for centuries, the living wood grown tall
and thickened with a hundred thousand days of light.

The old windmill creaks in perfect time
to the wind shaking the miles of pasture grass,
and the last farmhouse light goes off.

Something moves nearby. Coyotes hunt
these hills and packs of feral dogs.
But standing here at night accepts all that.

You are your own pale shadow in the quarter moon,
moving more slowly than the crippled stars,
part of the moonlight as the moonlight falls,

Part of the grass that answers the wind,
part of the midnight's watchfulness that knows
there is no silence but when danger comes.

IT'S A FACT

CALIFORNIA

Stanford University in Palo Alto was founded in memory of Leland Stanford, Jr. who died of typhoid fever just before his 16th birthday. The Stanfords dedicated the cornerstone of the non-denominational, co-educational university (unusual for the time) on May 14, 1887, the 19th anniversary of his birth.

※ ※ ※

The official state flower of California is the poppy; the state mammal is the grizzly bear; and the state tree (what else?) is the redwood.

The world's largest amphitheater is the Hollywood Bowl located in Hollywood, California.

※ ※ ※

The name "California" comes from a Spanish romance story called *Las Sergas de Esplandian*, in which a queen called Califa ruled a mythical Spanish island. When Spanish explorers first discovered California, they believed it to be an island and named it for the popular heroine.

Seabiscuit—the underdog California racehorse—became an inspiration to Americans during the great depression, ultimately beating War Admiral—the great east coast Triple Crown winner—in what many consider the greatest horse race in history.

⚜ ⚜ ⚜

The highest and lowest points in the lower 48 states are within 100 miles of each other in California: Mt. Whitney at 14,494 feet above sea level and Bad Water in Death Valley at 282 feet below sea level.

In 1958, columnist Herb Caen gave the name "beatnik" to the Beat Generation non-conformists. The "beatnik kit" was promoted by Vesuvio Café in San Francisco, where a list of notable Beats who had been booted out of the bar were engraved in the sidewalk outside the front door.

⚜ ⚜ ⚜

The hottest day in American history was in California's Death Valley on July 10, 1913. It was a sweltering 135°F!

BBQ Chicken Pizza

When California Pizza Kitchen first opened its Beverly Hills restaurant in 1985, they had a new concept of what pizza could be: everything you want, but with a twist. They claim to have created the Original BBQ Chicken Pizza, which has been replicated throughout the land. Since imitation is the sincerest form of flattery, we offer our own twist on this now California classic—enjoy the flavor of the West Coast no matter where you are. You may use premade pizza crust if making pizza crust seems too daunting.

1. In a small bowl, dissolve the honey in the warm water.

2. Sprinkle the yeast over the water and stir until it dissolves. Let the yeast mixture stand for 5 minutes, until a layer of foam forms on the surface.

3. In a large bowl, combine the flour and the salt. Make a well in the center of the flour mixture and pour the olive oil and the yeast mixture.

4. Stir the flour into the wet ingredients, until all the flour is incorporated. Adding more water if the dough seems too dry.

5. On a lightly floured surface, knead the dough for 15 minutes, until it is smooth and elastic. Shape the dough into a ball and put in a well-oiled bowl. Cover with a moist towel and let rise in a warm place until double in bulk (about $1\frac{1}{2}$ hours).

6. One hour before baking the pizzas, start preheating the oven with pizza stones inside at 500°F.

7. While oven is preheating and dough is rising, heat olive oil over medium-high heat, add chicken and cook until done (about 8 minutes).

8. Remove from heat. Coat chicken with 2 tablespoons barbecue sauce and place in refrigerator to cool slightly.

9. As chicken cools, move back to the dough. Punch dough down, and divide into 4 equal portions.

10. Roll out each portion into a 6- to 8-inch flat circle.

11. Spread $\frac{1}{4}$ cup barbecue sauce over the surface of each. Scatter cheese over the sauce followed by chicken and onion rings.

12. Place the pizza in the oven (on top of pizza stones). Bake until crust is crispy and cheese is bubbling (8-10 minutes).

13. Remove pizzas from the oven and garnish with chopped cilantro. Serve.

SERVES 4

1 tablespoon honey

1 cup warm water

2 teaspoons active dry yeast

3 cups all-purpose flour

1 teaspoon salt

1 tablespoon olive oil

10 ounces chicken breast, boned and skinned

2 tablespoons barbecue sauce

$\frac{1}{2}$ cup barbecue sauce

2 cups smoked Gouda

$\frac{1}{4}$ small red onion, sliced into rings

2 tablespoons cilantro

Sittin' in a park in Paris, France,
readin' the news and it sure looks bad.
They won't give peace a chance.
That was just a dream some of us had.
Still a lot of lands to see,
but I wouldn't wanna stay here.
It's too old and cold and settled in its ways here.
Ah, but California,
California comin' home.
I'm gonna see the folks I dig.
I'll even kiss a Sunset pig.
California I'm comin' home.

I met a red-neck on a Grecian Isle,
who did the "goat dance" very well.
He gave me back my smile,
but he kept my camera to sell…
Oh, the rogue, the red, red rogue.
He cooked good omelettes and stews,
And I might have stayed on with him there,
but my heart cried out for you
California, California,
oh, make me feel good, rock and roll band…
I'm your biggest fan…
California, I'm a-comin' home.

Chorus:
Oh, it gets so lonely,
when you're walkin' in a street so full of strangers.

All the news of home, you read,
just give you the blues,
just give you the blues.

So I bought me a ticket…
and caught a plane to Spain,
Went to a party down a red dirt road.
There were lots of pretty people there…
Reading Rollin' Stone, reading Vogue…
They said "How long can you hang around?"
I said, "A week, maybe two…
Just until my skin turns brown,
and then I'm going home to California,
California, I'm coming home…"
Oh, will you take me as I am?…
Strung out on another man.
California, I'm a-comin' home…

Chorus:
Oh, it gets so lonely,
when you're walkin' in a street so full of strangers.
All the news of home, you read,
just give you the blues,
just give you the blues.
So I read more about the war and the bloody
        changes oh, oh
Will you take me as I am,
will you take me as I am,
will you take me as I am.

CALIFORNIA

BY JONI MITCHELL

THE CALIFORNIA MISSIONS

A CHAIN OF 21 MISSIONS extend from San Diego, north through San Francisco, to Sonoma. The missions were settlements established by Spanish Catholic Franciscans to increase the Spanish presence in Alta California and convert the Native Americans to European Christian ways. The missionaries coerced local Native Americans to build and run the large ranches. In turn, the Spaniards introduced European religion, livestock, vegetables, fruits, and industry to the region.

During the 1600s, Jesuit priests built a system of self-sufficient missions along the coast of what is now southern California, on land laid claim to by the Spaniards. But the Spaniards began to fear that Russian settlements advancing down the Pacific Coast would threaten their lands. In 1767, King Juan Carlos III of Spain decided to remove the Jesuits and began colonizing areas further northward. Ranches were built near the sea to serve as suppliers for future Spanish ships. These large missionary farms were placed about 30 miles apart (or a long day's horse ride), and often along Native American trails, to make it easy for settlers to exchange goods and information, house travelers and convert Native Americans who walked the pathways. The road joining the missions became known as El Camino Real or "The King's Highway." This route remained a major north—south road until the 1920s, when much of it was incorporated into U.S. Highway 101.

The first nine missions were founded by Father Junipero Serra, beginning with the Mission San Diego de Alcala in 1769. When Father Serra died in 1784, Father Fermin Francisco Lasuén took over, originating the next nine. Other Franciscans established the final three missions, concluding in 1823 with the Mission San Francisco de Solano in Sonoma.

Native Americans who worked in the missions were taught the Spanish language and customs, as well as the Catholic religion. Though some were willing converts, many were not. When tribes approached the missions out of curiosity, they were often offered small gifts such as beads, blankets, and clothing in exchange for their labor. But once the Native Americans were inside the mission, most found they were not allowed to leave. Soldiers were posted at the missions to keep Native Americans from rebelling or escaping. Over the years, unconverted, resentful Native Americans attacked and raided various missions. In 1834, the Missions were officially secularized, and the Native Americans were allowed to return to their villages or stay on as ranch hands.

Most modern missions are active churches, and some have held services nonstop since they were originally constructed. Though many were damaged or destroyed in natural disasters, the missions have largely been rebuilt and retain prominent positions in California history. They were featured in Helen Hunt Jackson's romantic novel *Ramona* (1884) as well as in Hitchcock's film *Vertigo* (1958) and are hugely popular tourist attractions.

The most famous mission is Mission San Juan Capistrano, known throughout the world as the home of the swallows. Legend has it that the swallows first took refuge in the mission after their nests were destroyed by an angry local shopkeeper. Now every fall, on or around the Day of San Juan

(October 23rd), the swallows leave town in a flurried mass, flying 6,000 miles south to winter in Goya, Argentina. And every spring, on or around St. Joseph's Day (March 19th), the swallows return to their mud nests amongst the ruins of Mission San Juan Capistrano's church. Their annual return is marked by a jubilant festival that begins with bells ringing at the sight of the first swallow.

THE SILVERADO SQUATTERS

BY ROBERT LOUIS STEVENSON

A change in the color of the light usually called me in the morning. By a certain hour, the long, vertical chinks in our western gable, where the boards had shrunk and separated, flashed suddenly into my eyes as stripes of dazzling blue, at once so dark and splendid that I used to marvel how the qualities could be combined. At an earlier hour, the heavens in that quarter were still quietly colored, but the shoulder of the mountain which shuts in the canyon already glowed with sunlight in a wonderful compound of gold and rose and green; and this too would kindle, although more mildly and with rainbow tints, the fissures of our crazy gable. If I were sleeping heavily, it was the bold blue that struck me awake; if more lightly, then I would come to myself in that earlier and fairer light.

One Sunday morning, about five, the first brightness called me. I rose and turned to the east, not for my devotions, but for air. The night had been very still. The little private gale that blew every evening in our canyon, for ten minutes or perhaps a quarter of an hour, had swiftly blown itself out; in the hours that followed not a sigh of wind had shaken the treetops; and our barrack, for all its breaches, was less fresh that morning than of wont. But I had no sooner reached the window than I forgot all else in the sight that met my eyes, and I made but two bounds into my clothes, and down the crazy plank to the platform.

The sun was still concealed below the opposite hilltops, though it was shining already, not twenty feet above my head, on our own mountain slope. But the scene, beyond a few near features, was entirely changed. Napa Valley was gone; gone were all the lower slopes and woody foothills of the range; and in their place, not a thousand feet below me, rolled a great level ocean.

It was as though I had gone to bed the night before, safe in a nook of inland mountains, and had awakened in a bay upon the coast. I had seen these inundations from below; at Calistoga I had risen and gone abroad in the early morning, coughing and sneezing, under fathoms on fathoms of gray sea vapor, like a cloudy sky—a dull sight for the artist, and a painful experience for the invalid. But to sit aloft one's self in the pure air and under the unclouded dome of heaven, and thus look down on the submergence of the valley, was strangely different and even delightful to the eyes. Far away were hilltops like little islands. Nearer, a smoky surf beat about the foot of precipices and poured into all the coves of these rough mountains. The color of that fog ocean was a thing never to be forgotten. For an instant, among the Hebrides and just about sundown, I have seen something like it on the sea itself. But the white was not so opaline; nor was there, what surprisingly increased the effect, that breathless, crystal stillness cover all. Even in its gentlest moods the salt sea travails, moaning among the weeks or lisping on the sand; but that vast fog ocean lay in a trance of silence, nor did the sweet air of the morning tremble with a sound.

As I continued to sit upon the dump, I began to observe that this sea was not so level as at first sight it appeared to be. Away in the extreme south, a little hill of fog arose against the sky above the general surface, and as it had already caught the sun, it shone on the horizon like the topsails of some giant ship. There were huge waves, stationary, as it seemed, like waves in a frozen sea; and yet, as I looked again, I was not sure but they were moving after all, with a slow and august advance. And while I was yet doubting, a promontory of the hills some four or five miles away, conspicuous by a bouquet of tall pines, was in a single instant overtaken and swallowed up. It reappeared in a little, with its pines, but this time as an islet, and only to be swallowed up once more and then for good. This set me looking nearer, and I saw that in every cove along the line of mountains the fog was being piled in higher and higher, as though by some wind that was inaudible to me. I could trace its progress, one pine tree first growing hazy and then disappearing after another; although sometimes there was none of this fore-running haze, but the whole opaque white ocean gave a start and swallowed a piece of mountain at a gulp. It was to flee these poisonous fogs that I had left the seaboard, and climbed so high among the mountains. And now, behold, here came the fog to besiege me in my chosen altitudes, and yet came so beautifully that my first thought was of welcome.

The sun had now gotten much higher, and through all the gaps of the hills it cast long bars of gold across that white ocean. An eagle, or some other very great bird of the mountain, came wheeling over the nearer pine-tops, and hung, poised and something sideways, as if to look abroad on that unwonted desolation, spying, perhaps with terror, for the aeries of her comrades. Then, with a long cry, she disappeared again towards Lake County and the clearer air. At length it seemed to me as if the flood were beginning to subside. The old landmarks, by whose disappearance I had measured its advance, here a crag, there a brave pine tree, now began, in the inverse order, to make their reappearance into daylight. I judged all danger of the fog was over. This was not Noah's flood; it was but a morning spring, and would now drift out seaward whence it came. So, mightily relieved, and a good deal exhilarated by the light, I went into the house to light the fire.

Here is a climate that breeds vigor, with just sufficient geniality to prevent the expenditure of most of that vigor in fighting the elements.

—Jack London

FROM THE SONG MT. TAMALPAIS SINGS

BY LEW WELCH

This is the last place.
There is nowhere else to go.
This is why
once again we celebrate the
Headland's huge, cairn-studded fall
into the sea.

ARRIVING BY THE PANAMA STEAMER, I stopped one day in San Francisco and then inquired for the nearest way out of town. "But where do you want to go?" asked the man to whom I had applied for this important information. "To any place that is wild," I said. This reply startled him. He seemed to fear I might be crazy and therefore the sooner I was out of town the better, so he directed me to the Oakland ferry.

FROM THE WONDERS OF YOSEMITE

BY JOHN MUIR

So on the first of April, 1868, I set out afoot for Yosemite. It was the bloom-time of the year over the lowlands and coast ranges; the landscapes of the Santa Clara Valley were fairly drenched with sunshine, all the air was quivering with the songs of the meadow-larks, and the hills were so covered with flowers that they seemed to be painted. Slow indeed was my progress through these glorious gardens, the first of the California flora I had seen. Cattle and cultivation were making few scars as yet, and I wandered enchanted in long wavering curves, knowing by my pocket map that Yosemite Valley lay to the east and that I should surely find it.

Looking eastward from the summit of the Pacheco Pass one shining morning, a landscape was displayed that after all my wanderings still appears as the most beautiful I have ever beheld. At my feet lay the Great Central Valley of California, level and flowery, like a lake of pure sunshine, forty or fifty miles wide, five hundred miles long, one rich furred garden of yellow Compositae. And from the eastern boundary of this vast golden flower-bed rose the mighty Sierra, miles in height, and so gloriously colored and so radiant, it seemed not clothed with light, but wholly composed of it, like the wall of some celestial city.

Along the top and extending a good way down, was a rich pearl-gray belt of snow; below it a belt of blue and dark purple, marking the extension of the forests; and stretching along the base of the range a broad belt of rose-purple; all these colors, from the blue sky to the yellow valley smoothly blending as they do in a rainbow, making a wall of light ineffably fine.

Then it seemed to me that the Sierra should be called, not the Nevada or Snowy Range, but the Range of Light. And after ten years of wandering and wondering in the heart of it, rejoicing in its glorious floods of light, the white beams of the morning streaming through the passes, the noonday radiance on the crystal rocks, the flush of the alpenglow, and the irised spray of countless waterfalls, it still seems above all others the Range of Light.

In general views no mark of man is visible upon it, nor anything to suggest the wonderful depth and grandeur of its sculpture....Nevertheless the whole range five hundred miles long is furrowed with cañons 2,000 to 5,000 feet deep, in which once flowed majestic glaciers, and in which now flow and sing the bright rejoicing rivers....

The most famous and accessible of these cañon valleys, and also the one that presents their most striking and sublime features on the grandest scale, is the Yosemite, situated in the basin of the Merced River at an elevation of 4,000 feet above the level of the sea. It is about seven miles long, half a mile to a mile wide, and nearly a mile deep in the solid granite flank of the range. The walls are made up of rocks, mountains in size, partly separated from each other by side cañons, and they are so sheer in front, and so compactly and harmoniously arranged on a level floor, that the Valley, comprehensively seen, looks like an immense hall or temple lighted from above.

But no temple made with hands can compare with Yosemite. Every rock in its walls seems to glow with life. Some lean back in majestic repose; others, absolutely sheer or nearly so for thousands of feet,

advance beyond their companions in thoughtful attitudes, giving welcome to storms and calms alike, seemingly aware, yet heedless, of everything going on about them. Awful in stern, immovable majesty, how softly these rocks are adorned, and how fine and reassuring the company they keep: their feet among beautiful groves and meadows, their brows in the sky, a thousand flowers leaning confidingly against their feet, bathed in floods of water, floods of light, while the snow and waterfalls, the winds and avalanches and clouds shine and sing and wreathe about them as the years go by, and myriads of small winged creatures—birds, bees, butterflies—give glad animation and help to make all the air into music.

Down through the middle of the Valley flows the crystal Merced, River of Mercy, peacefully quiet, reflecting lilies and trees and the onlooking rocks; things frail and fleeting and types of endurance meeting here and blending in countless forms, as if into this one mountain mansion Nature had gathered her choicest treasures, to draw her lovers into close and confiding communion with her.

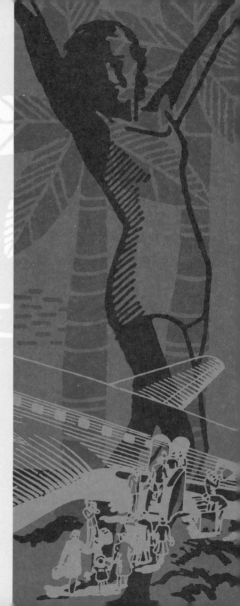

THE GREAT OUTDOORS: CALIFORNIA'S NATIONAL PARKS

The Channel Islands National Park consists of five remote unpopulated islands off the coast—Anacapa, Santa Cruz, Santa Rosa, San Miguel, and Santa Barbara—stretching from just north of Ventura to just south of Los Angeles.

⚬ ⚬ ⚬

The Channel Islands are home to over 2,000 species of wildlife—145 of which are found no where else in the world—and are surrounded by a marine sanctuary that protects thousands of species of sea life and houses a giant kelp forest.

Death Valley contains the hottest, driest, and lowest points in America. It got its name from lost pioneers, ultimately rescued, who had believed they would not survive this inhospitable site.

⚬ ⚬ ⚬

More than 1.2 million people each year visit Death Valley's rolling hills, golden sand dunes, lush tropical oases, and more than 900 species of plants and animals.

⚬ ⚬ ⚬

Named for its giant yucca trees, Joshua Tree National Park is bound by two distinct desert ecosystems: the hotter, drier lowlands of the Colorado, and the wetter, cooler Mojave highlands.

❀ ❀ ❀

Joshua Tree National Park has more than 500 archeological sites and 88 historic structures, as well as five spring-fed oases covered in fan palms.

❀ ❀ ❀

The Joshua tree is the only tree that grows in California's Mojave Desert.

❀ ❀ ❀

Sequoia and Kings Canyon—separately founded but jointly administered—is a "superpark," 66 miles long and 36 miles across at its widest point. It contains the gravity defying stalactites of both Crystal Cave and Cedar Grove, which John Muir once called a "rival of Yosemite."

❀ ❀ ❀

A hiker can retreat further into nature (and away from roads) in Sequoia and Kings Canyon than anywhere else in the country *and* enjoy the amazing spectacle of the oldest trees on earth, the sequoias.

❇ ❇ ❇

The California redwoods—coast redwoods and giant sequoia—are the tallest and largest living organisms in the world.

❇ ❇ ❇

Yosemite National Park is visited by more than 4 million people a year. Hikers can find solitude in the breathtaking mountain vistas or join the multitude of visitors in the valley (over 14,000 on any given summer day).

❇ ❇ ❇

Established in 1890, Yosemite National Park is the home to Yosemite Falls (the highest falls in North America), the massive cliffs of El Capitan, and the grandeur of Mariposa Grove (the largest grouping of sequoias in the park).

❇ ❇ ❇

Made up of Jedediah Smith, Del Norte Coast, and Prairie Creek state parks, the Redwood National Park encompasses 45% of all of the old-growth redwood trees in California.

❇ ❇ ❇

The tallest living things on Earth were in danger of being logged out of existence not so long ago, and in 1978 Congress added 48,000 acres to Redwood, including 36,000 acres that had already been clear cut.

❇ ❇ ❇

The quiet forests and crystal-clear lakes of Lassen Volcanic National Park belie the fire that lurks beneath their surface. Formed by eruptions from the ancient volcanano Mt. Tehama, Lassen has been sleeping since 1921, but the thermal steam rising from the ground, bubbling mud pools, and new growth on the devastated landscape draws nearly a half million visitors a year.

TREE

BY JANE HIRSHFIELD

It is foolish
to let a young redwood
grow next to a house.

Even in this
one lifetime,
you will have to choose.

That great calm being,
this clutter of soup pots and books—

Already the first branch-tips brush at the window.
Softly, calmly, immensity taps at your life.

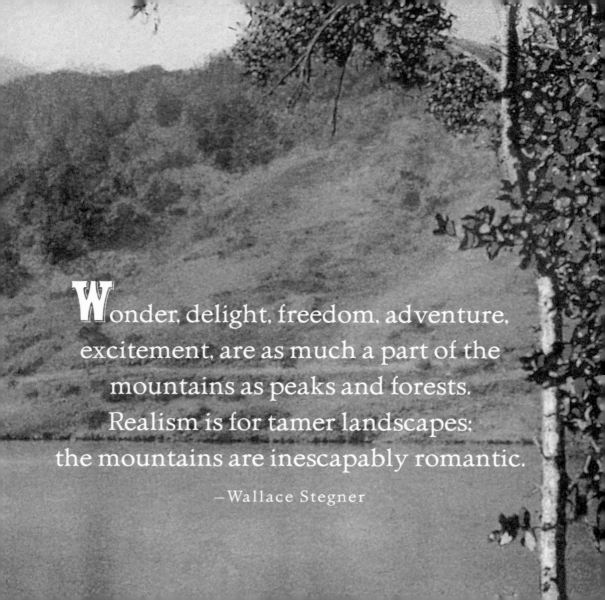

Wonder, delight, freedom, adventure,
excitement, are as much a part of the
mountains as peaks and forests.
Realism is for tamer landscapes;
the mountains are inescapably romantic.

—Wallace Stegner

Brown Rice Pudding with California Raisins

CALIFORNIA IS KNOWN FOR ITS RAISINS, YET ITS FIRST CROP OF THIS CHEWY, SWEET FRUIT WAS PROBABLY A MISTAKE. IN THE LATE 1800S, FARMERS IN THE SAN JOAQUIN VALLEY ENCOUNTERED A MAJOR HEAT WAVE THAT CAUSED THEIR GRAPES TO DIE ON THE VINE BEFORE THEY COULD BE HARVESTED. LUCKILY, THEY DISCOVERED THAT THE DRIED GRAPES WERE STILL DELICIOUS, AND NOW THE SAN JOAQUIN VALLEY PRODUCES ABOUT HALF OF THE WORLD'S SUPPLY OF RAISINS. THESE DAYS, GRAPES ARE PICKED RIPE AND LAID OUT IN THE CALIFORNIA SUN TO DRY FOR AS LONG AS THREE WEEKS. CALIFORNIA RAISINS GIVE THIS BROWN RICE PUDDING THE PERFECT AMOUNT OF SWEETNESS.

1. In a large saucepan, bring the rice, milk, raisins, vanilla bean and scrapings, candied ginger, orange zest, and one cup of sugar to a simmer on low heat.

2. Cover, and stirring occasionally, simmer for 35-40 minutes, or until rice is tender.

3. Remove pot from heat and add egg yolks, stirring constantly until the mixture is thick and creamy.

4. Place warm rice pudding in serving dishes, cover tightly and refrigerate until cool (at least 2 hours or overnight). Serve.

OPTIONAL GARNISH:

1. When ready to serve, place remaining cup of sugar in a small skillet over medium-high heat.

2. Cook sugar until it turns a deep-caramel color.

   While sugar is cooking, remove rice pudding from refrigerator. Top with whipped cream.

3. Once sugar has finished caramelizing, carefully drizzle over the whipped cream-topped rice pudding. Serve.

SERVES 4

Ingredients

1 cup brown rice

5 cups milk

1/2 cup California raisins

1/4 cup golden raisins

1 vanilla bean, split lengthwise and scraped

2 tablespoons candied ginger, chopped

1 orange, zested

1 cup sugar

4 egg yolks, lightly beaten

1 additional cup sugar, optional

Whipped cream, for garnish, optional

Hooray for Hollywood!
That screwy ballyhooey Hollywood,
Where any office boy or young mechanic
can be a panic, with just a good looking pan,
And any barmaid can be a star maid,
If she dances with or without a fan.

Hooray for Hollywood!
Where you're terrific if you're even good,
Where anyone at all from Shirley Temple
to Aimee Semple is equally understood,
Go out and try your luck,
You might be Donald Duck!
Hooray for Hollywood!

Hooray for Hollywood!
That phony super Coney Hollywood,
They come from Chillicothes and Paducahs
with their bazookas to get their names up in
   lights,
All armed with photos from local rotos,
With their hair in ribbons and legs in tights.

Hooray for Hollywood!
You may be homely in your neighborhood,
But if you think that you can be an actor,
see Mister Factor, he'd make a monkey look
   good,
Within a half an hour,
You'll look like Tyrone Power!
Hooray for Hollywood!

HOORAY FOR
HOLLYWOOD

Lyrics by Johnny Mercer

HOLLYWOOD IS MUCH MORE than a place. It is a word that conjures up images of the glamorous, and sometimes seedy, universe of movies, entertainment, and celebrities. But moviemaking didn't start there. It, like so many Californians, is a transplant. Movie cameras were first developed in America and Europe in the 1890s, and by

LIGHTS, CAMERA, ACTION! HOLLYWOOD

the turn of the century, the first movies were being produced in New York City and Chicago. In 1908, because competition was fierce, rules were few, and piracy was pervasive, the 10 largest production companies banded together to control the industry, often enforcing their dominance by ransacking other studios.

In defiance of the East Coast bullies, independent filmmakers moved to California, drawn to its plentiful space, willing workers, beautiful landscapes, reliable climate, and nonstop sunshine. In 1911, the Nestor Company opened Hollywood's first film studio. By 1915, the courts had busted the East Coast monopoly and new "indie" studios, such as Universal, Paramount, and Fox, began setting up shop around Los Angeles in "Hollywoodland." To cement their control of not only production and distribution, but also exhibition, studios began buying theaters around the country.

In the beginning, short, documentary-like "picture shows" were shown after vaudeville acts as a way of chasing people out. But movie storytelling quickly evolved. *The Life of an American Fireman* (1903) depicted a character's thoughts, and *The Great Train Robbery* (1903) used jumps in time to skip nonessential events. Legendary director D.W. Griffith began making long, serious films using close-ups to increase intimacy, panoramic shots to reveal a film's environment, and editing techniques such as fades and dissolves to symbolize characters' mental states. Mack Sennett made people laugh drawing on slapstick, his crazy Keystone cops, and the talents of young vaudevillian performer Charlie Chaplin.

By the late 1920s, Hollywood was churning out movies at an outlandish pace. High-powered producers, such as Adolph Zukor, Louis B. Mayer, and Samuel Goldwyn, dominated the industry. In 1927, the Motion Picture Academy of Arts and Sciences launched an annual award ceremony (later nicknamed the Oscars) that upped the reputation and exposure of the industry. But the release of *The Jazz Singer* (1927), the first feature-length film with synchronous sound, turned Hollywood on its ear, marking the death of silent pictures and the ruin of many silent film stars whose voices didn't live up to their dazzling images.

During the Great Depression of the 1930s, movie attendance was almost three times higher than it is today. In 1938, more than 80 million people per week went to the movies. Studios answered the incredible demand by perfecting their factory-like system, controlling the financing, screenwriting, directing, editing, and distribution, and making formula film after formula film. Much like theater companies, studios chose actors from groups they already employed. Major studios became known for certain specialties: MGM for its stars (Greta Garbo, Clark Gable, Jimmy Stewart); Paramount for its writers and directors (Billy Wilder, Cecil B. DeMille); RKO for its musicals (starring Fred Astaire and Ginger Rogers), comedies (starring Cary Grant), B-movies (*Cat People*, 1942), and thought-provoking fare (*Citizen Kane*, 1941); Fox for its adventure and historical movies; Universal for its horror classics (*Frankenstein*, 1931, *Dracula*, 1931); and Warner Bros. for its gangster movies (*Scarface*, 1932), biographies (*The Life of Emile Zola*, 1937), and musicals (Busby Berkley's movies). Majestic movie palaces and suburban drive-ins were erected all across the United States. At its peak in 1946, the industry grossed nearly $2 billion.

But in 1948, the courts ruled that studios could no longer both make movies and own the exhibiting theaters. The studios were also wrangling with national politics and the new, popular medium of television. The House Un-American Activities Committee, formed in 1947, set out to expose Hollywood's communist sympathizers. And for over 10 years, Hollywood's self-imposed blacklist kept many entertainment professionals from working or, at the very least, from getting proper screen credit.

To compete with TV, the studios premiered flashy, new technologies, such as Smell-O-Vision, 3-D, and CinemaScope. New revenue streams opened up in 1956, when Hollywood inked a deal that allowed studios to broadcast old movies on television. But 1962 saw only $900 million in box-office receipts, and by 1968 little more than 20 million people per week were turning out for movies. To save money, the studios stopped renewing contracts and began hiring independent cast and crew for each film (as they still do.) Many cite the mammoth-budget failure *Cleopatra* (1963) as the film that marked the collapse of the old-studio system.

Movies of the 1950s and '60s traded razzle dazzle for a grittier realism and independent filmmakers began to make their mark. A spate of science fiction, rock 'n' roll, and horror films were aimed at adolescents. Rejecting traditional celebrity glitz, younger audiences responded to anti-heroes and edgy depictions of sex and violence. Art films from Europe made people hungry for more intellectual fodder. Embracing previously underground forms of moviemaking, Hollywood produced films such as *The Graduate* (1967), *Bonnie and Clyde* (1968), and *Easy Rider* (1969). People returned to the theaters, and subsequently, the 1970s marked the rise of many great filmmakers, including Robert Altman (*M*A*S*H*, 1970), Francis Ford Coppola (*The Godfather*, 1972), and Martin Scorsese (*Taxi Driver*, 1973).

When Steven Spielberg's *Jaws* (1975) grossed over $100 million by appealing to men and women of all ages, the paradigm again shifted. Filmmakers were pushed to make spectacle films aimed at the widest possible audience. Blockbusters such as *Raiders of the Lost Ark* (1981) and *E.T.* (1982) were hugely successful. Special effects showcased in films such as *Star Wars* (1977) were increasingly relied on, and their quality improved dramatically. In the 1980s, the film industry profited from the proliferation of cheaper VCRs and the easing of government regulations separating production and distribution. As drive-ins fell into disrepair, indoor movie multiplexes sprang up in cities and suburbs. Burgeoning cable companies offered new avenues of entertainment that encouraged more independent productions.

Though the recession of the early 1990s affected box-office revenues, sales picked up again by 1993. And while mainstream, big-budget, special effects-laden films were still the rage, independent filmmakers began proving they could compete with the studios. African-American filmmakers such as Spike Lee (*Mo' Better Blues*, 1990) and John Singleton (*Boyz N the Hood*, 1991), female directors such as Nora Ephron (*Sleepless in Seattle*, 1993), and female writers such as Calli Khouri (*Thelma and Louise*, 1991) made names for themselves. Hollywood tried make money while tackling serious themes such as AIDS (*Philadelphia*, 1993) and the Holocaust (*Schindler's List*, 1993). But stars' salaries, agency fees, production costs, and marketing expenses soared. Studios looking for sure-fire hits produced more and more high-speed action-thrillers, remakes, re-releases, and sequels. Nevertheless, independent studios produced four of the five Best Picture nominees in 1996.

As we begin the 21st Century, Hollywood seems to be entering the digital age. *The Matrix* trilogy's (1993, 1999, 2003) use of computer-generated images revolutionized the action-movie genre. *Finding Nemo* (2003) was an extremely successful, entirely computer-generated animated film. And *The Lord of the Rings* trilogy (2001, 2002, 2003) skillfully incorporated cutting-edge digital effects, helping them snag a total of 17 Oscars. But whatever is in store—and despite the fact that most studios have moved from Hollywood-proper to nearby areas—"Hollywood" remains the American film industry's symbolic heart and soul.

CALIFORNIA CONFIDENTIAL

In January of 1947, the body of aspiring actress Elizabeth Short was found severed into two. Her death was dubbed "The Black Dahlia Murder" due to her jet-black hair and black clothes. Short's address book (with one page removed) and her birth certificate were sent by her killer to the LAPD. More than 50 people confessed to the murder, and to this day there are still new theories and investigations, but the case has never been closed

On August 4, 1962, at age 36, actress Marilyn Monroe was found dead in her Brentwood bungalow, an apparent victim of suicide by barbiturate overdose. However, many continue to speculate on the true cause of her death.

California's most elusive serial killer is suspected of killing 49 victims—including 39 women—in northern California between October 1966 and May 1981. The Zodiac Killer is famous for writing 21 letters to local press and police explaining that he was killing to "collect slaves," to serve him in the after-life. The case remains open to this day.

Claiming to get his instruction from the Beatles' song, "Helter Skelter," Charles Manson led a satanic cult in the late '60s, whose members or "creepy crawlers" traveled California committing random, ritualistic killings. They are best known for the murder of actress Sharon Tate, Roman Polanksi's pregnant wife. Even after his imprisonment in 1969, Manson followers continued to terrorize Californians well into the '70s.

❆ ❆ ❆

Patty Hearst, granddaughter of legendary newspaper publisher William Randolph Hearst, was kidnapped at gunpoint in Berkeley in February 1974. Claiming to belong to the Symbionese Liberation Army (SLA), they demanded food for the poor as ransom. Her family paid, but two months later Patty—who claimed she had been tortured and brainwashed—aided the group in a San Francisco bank robbery. Caught and sent to jail for 35 years, her sentence was later shortened to seven years.

❆ ❆ ❆

The Night Stalker terrorized Los Angeles in June of 1984 by entering homes through unlocked doors and windows and torturing his victims to death. In just three weeks, he claimed at least 16 lives before being caught and revealed as Richard Ramirez. He was sentenced to death in November 1989, and told reporters, "I'll see you all at Disneyland." Ramirez is currently on San Quentin's death row.

❆ ❆ ❆

In a 133-day televised trial that captivated America and the world, Orenthal James Simpson, the football-star-turned-sports-announcer, was found not guilty of murdering his ex-wife Nicole Brown and her friend Ronald Goldman in 1995. However, in a civil trial two years later, O.J. *was* found liable in both deaths and ordered to pay the Goldman family $8.5 million. Brown and Goldman were found brutally stabbed outside her Brentwood condominium the night of June 12, 1994.

❆ ❆ ❆

In January 1976, adopted cousins Ken Bianchi and Angelo Buono became the "Hillside Stranglers." In two months they abducted and killed ten women in Los Angeles, frequently leaving the dead, naked bodies displayed on the highway embankments and hillsides of the crime scene. They captured their victims by impersonating policemen and stopping female motorists or nabbing prostitutes, and subjected them to torture, sexual assault, and brutality before strangling them. Buono died in prison in September 2002. Bianchi is still in prison.

❈ ❈ ❈

In the 1930s, Benjamin "Bugsy" Siegel arrived from New York to become the Syndicate's Los Angeles Mafia Boss. He hobnobbed with such celebrities Jean Harlow, Clark Gable, Gary Cooper, and Cary Grant while convincing the mob to invest $6 million to build a Las Vegas casino, the Flamingo. But a hit was ordered on him when the casino was an initial flop and Bugsy was suspected of skimming money off the top. Bugsy was murdered at the home of longtime lover Virginia Hill in Beverly Hills in 1947.

❈ ❈ ❈

Leonard Lake and Charles Ng built a torture chamber and snuff film parlor in a remote northern California ranch. Lake was caught in June, 1985, took a cyanide pill, and died four days later. Ng escaped but

was arrested a month later. Police discovered the remains of up to 25 men, women, and children who been sexually assaulted, murdered, burned, and scattered on Lake's property. After a trial that cost the state more than $10 million (the most expensive in its history), Ng now sits on California's death row.

SHANGRI-LA

BY SUZANNE LUMMIS

*In New York they think all of
California is like L.A. And they
think everyone in L.A. has a maid.
And they don't believe you if you
try to tell them.*
       —Radio talk show caller

It's true, here we are all blonde,
even in the dark, on Mondays
or in slow traffic.

Even in our off-guard moments,
startled by a passer-by,
we are young.

Here we are all privileged,
even in our sleep. At night
the maids hover like sweetly

tranquilized angels over
the glazed or enameled surface
of things, purring *clean clean*…

It's all true. We girls sip lemon-lime through a straw,
make love, Revlon our nails.
We take our long sleek legs out for a walk,
let them catch light.

When someone snaps, "Get real!"
it hurts us, real pain like we've seen
in the news. So we throw beach robes
over our tans, and cruise down the boulevard
tossing Lifesavers into our mouths,
car radios singing *am*.

New York is it true
that in the rest of the world it is winter?

Our state is a mosaic of blue pools,
even the Mojave, and the palm trees
line up straight to the Sierra Nevadas,
And the surf comes down slow like
delirious laundry, even near Fresno.

New York, is it true that great cold
makes the bones ache as if broken?

We're sorry we can't be reached
by plane or bus, sorry one can't pull
even the tiniest thing out of a dream.
We're like the landscape inside
a plastic dome filled with water.

But turn us over, then upright.
See?
No snow falls.

Cobb Salad

SALAD:

2 chicken breasts,
bones in, skin on

3 eggs

8 slices bacon
(to be truly California chic,
substitute turkey bacon)

1 head lettuce
(Iceberg is traditionally used
but you may try any variation
including romaine, arugula,
watercress, or Boston butter.)

2 tomatoes,
seeded and chopped

³/₄ cup blue cheese, crumbled

1 avocado, peeled,
pitted, and diced

¹/₂ cup chopped green onion

DRESSING:

¹/₂ cup mayonnaise

¹/₄ cup sour cream

¹/₂ cup crumbled blue cheese

1 clove garlic, finely minced

2 tablespoons
flat-leaf parsley, minced

2 tablespoons white vinegar

THE BROWN DERBY RESTAURANT IN LOS ANGELES GENERALLY GETS THE CREDIT FOR INVENTING THIS CALIFORNIA FAVORITE. AS THE STORY GOES, IN 1937 BOB COBB, THE RESTAURANT'S MANAGER, WAS HUNGRY AFTER A LONG SHIFT AND PROWLING THE KITCHEN FOR SOMETHING TO EAT. HE GRABBED SOME LETTUCE, AN AVOCADO, SOME TOMATOES, A COLD BREAST OF CHICKEN, A FEW HARD BOILED EGGS, A BIT OF CHEESE, AND SOME CRISPY BACON AND TOPPED IT WITH SOME FRENCH DRESSING. HIS THROWN-TOGETHER DISH WAS DELICIOUS AND SOON BECAME A FAVORITE OF SID GRAUMAN, OWNER OF GRAUMAN'S CHINESE THEATER. THE SALAD MADE ITS WAY ONTO THE BROWN DERBY'S MENU, AND SINCE 1937, THE RESTAURANT HAS SOLD OVER FOUR MILLION COBB SALADS! OUR VERSION WILL BRING YOU RIGHT BACK TO OLD HOLLYWOOD WITH THE TASTE CALIFORNIANS HAVE LOVED FOR DECADES.

1. Preheat oven to 350°F. Generously salt and pepper chicken breasts. Roast for 40 minutes. Allow chicken to cool before skinning and chopping meat into bite-size pieces.

2. While breasts cool, place eggs in a saucepan and cover completely with cold water. Bring water to a boil. Cover, remove from heat, and let eggs stand in hot water for 10 to 12 minutes. Carefully remove from hot water, cool, peel, and finely chop.

3. Place bacon in a large skillet. Cook over medium-high heat until brown and crisp. Drain on paper towels, crumble, and set aside.

4. Combine mayonnaise, sour cream, blue cheese, garlic, parsley, and vinegar in a large bowl.

BEVERLY HILLS BROWN DERBY — 9537 WILSHIRE BLVD. — BEVERLY HILLS, CALIF.

5. Divide lettuce onto 2 plates and drizzle generously with dressing, reserving any extra to be served on the side.

6. Evenly divide and arrange chicken, eggs, tomatoes, blue cheese, bacon, avocado, and green onions in a row on top of the lettuce. Serve.

SERVES 2

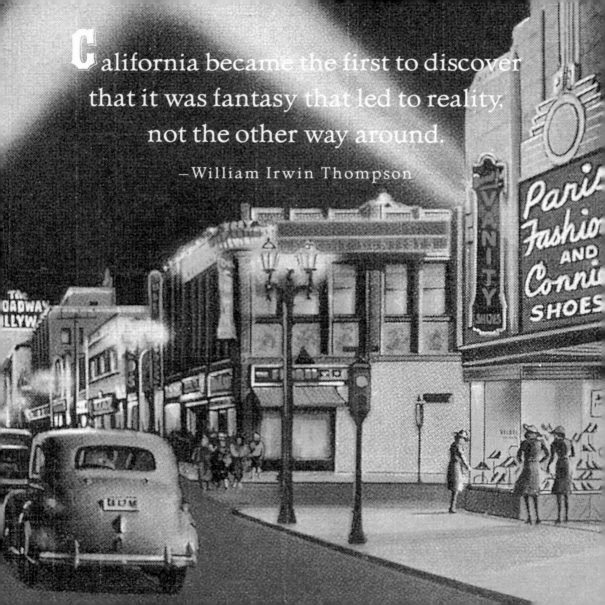

California became the first to discover that it was fantasy that led to reality, not the other way around.

—William Irwin Thompson

FROM THE WHITE ALBUM
BY JOAN DIDION

To understand what was going on it is perhaps necessary to have participated in the freeway experience, which is the only secular communion Los Angeles has. Mere driving on the freeway is in no way the same as participating in it. Anyone can "drive" on the freeway, and many people with no vocation for it do, hesitating here and resisting there, losing the rhythm of the lane change, thinking about where they came from and where they are going. Actual participants think only about where they are. Actual participation requires a total surrender, a concentration so intense as to seem a kind of narcosis, a rapture-of-the-freeway. The mind goes clean. The rhythm takes over. A distortion of time occurs, the same distortion that characterizes the instant before an accident. It takes only a few seconds to get off the Santa Monica Freeway at National-Overland, which is a difficult exit requiring the driver to cross two new lanes of traffic streamed in from the San Diego Freeway, but those few second always seem to me the longest part of the trip. The moment is dangerous. The exhilaration is in doing it. "As you acquire the special skills involved," Reyner Banham observed in an extraordinary chapter about the freeways in his 1971 *Los Angeles: The Architecture of Four Ecologies*, "the freeways become a special way of being alive...the extreme concentration required in Los Angeles seems to bring on a state of heightened awareness that some locals find mystical."

MONEY IS THE ROOT

AS A WRITER IN HOLLYWOOD, I spent more time arguing than writing—until the last four years when the British boycott left me without much bargaining power. My chief memory of movieland is one of asking in the producer's office why must I change the script, eviscerate it, cripple and hamstring it? Why must I strip the hero of his few semi-intelligent remarks and why must I tack on a corny ending that makes the stomach shudder? Half of all the movie writers argue in this fashion. The other half writhe in silence, and the psychoanalyst's couch or the liquor bottle claim them both.

ARTIST, FRIEND, AND MONEYMAKER

BY BEN HECHT

Before it might seem that I am writing about a tribe of Shelleys in chains, I should make it clear that the movie writers "ruined" by the movies are for the most part a run of greedy hacks and incompetent thickheads. Out of the thousand writers huffing and puffing through movieland there are scarcely fifty men and women of wit or talent. The rest of the fraternity is deadwood. Yet, in a curious way, there is not much difference between

the product of a good writer and a bad one. They both have to toe the same mark.

Nor are the bad writers better off spiritually. Their way is just as thorny. Minus talent or competence, the need for self-expression churns foolishly in them and their hearts throw themselves in a wild pitch for fame. And no less than the literary elite of Hollywood they feel the string of its knout. However cynical, overpaid, or inept you are, it is impossible to create entertainment without feeling the urges that haunt creative work. The artist's ego, even the ego of the Hollywood hack, must always jerk around a bit under restraint.

The studio bosses are not too inconvenienced by this bit of struggle. Experience has proved that the Hollywood artist in revolt is usually to be brought to heel by a raise in salary. My own discontent with what I was asked to do in Hollywood was so loud that I finally received a hundred and twenty-five thousand dollars for four weeks of script writing.

HOLLYWOOD

❊ ❊ ❊

Charlie Chaplin, Hollywood's silent comedian with the trademark splay-footed walk, had his feet insured for $150,000 in the 1920s—a fortune at the time.

❊ ❊ ❊

Alfred Hitchcock bought the rights to *Psycho* anonymously from novelist Robert Bloch for just $9,000. He then bought up as many copies of the novel as he could to keep the ending a secret.

❊ ❊ ❊

The world-famous Hollywood sign was built in 1926 to advertise a prestigious new housing subdivision. It originally read "Hollywoodland."

❊ ❊ ❊

In 1978, the Hollywood sign was rebuilt at a cost of $28,000 per letter. The new and improved sign stands 45 feet high, 450 feet long, and weighs 480,000 pounds!

❊ ❊ ❊

The first 1,558 stars on the "Hollywood Walk of Fame" were installed in 1960, with Joanne Woodward receiving the very first star! Since then, about two new stars are added per month. Each one is made from pink terrazzo and brass.

❊ ❊ ❊

Ever wonder what some of your favorite film stars' favorite films are?

Madonna loves *To Kill A Mockingbird*; Halle Berry's first choice is *Thelma & Louise*; Jackie Chan likes *The Sound of Music*; Tim Robbins likes *Waiting for Guffman*; and Robert Duvall's pick is *My Life as a Dog*—just to name a few.

❈ ❈ ❈

Numerous fictional characters have stars on the "Walk," including Lassie, Rin Tin Tin, Mickey Mouse, Bugs Bunny, Woody Woodpecker, Snow White, Big Bird, and Donald Duck.

❈ ❈ ❈

The person awarded the most total Oscars over his lifetime was Walt Disney. The grand total was 26 statuettes!

❈ ❈ ❈

In 1999, a bedazzling Whoopi Goldberg wore $41 million worth of Elizabethan jewels to the Academy Awards, on loan from Harry Winston. The ensemble, which included a $15 million diamond ring, was the most valuable collection ever worn to the Oscars.

❈ ❈ ❈

Hollywood's longest Oscar acceptance speech was given by Greer Garson in 1942, when she won Best Actress for *Mrs. Miniver*. It lasted over five minutes.

❈ ❈ ❈

The legendary footprints outside of the Mann Chinese Theater were actually started by accident! Silent film star Norma Talmadge started the trend when she mistakenly stepped in wet cement while visiting the newly built theater.

❈ ❈ ❈

The mechanical shark for Steven Spielberg's *Jaws* (1975) wasn't water tested during construction. When it was finally put in the water in Martha's Vineyard for shooting, it sank straight to the ocean floor! A team of divers had to retrieve it.

❈ ❈ ❈

During World War II, metal was scarce, so the Academy awarded plaster statuettes on Oscar night. After the war, winners exchanged them for the traditional gold-plated statues.

I can see it all now. I will never forget
what you meant to me. Don't have a
    single regret.
And I was feelin' alright
when it was just me and you.
We loved with all of our might.
That's all we wanted to do.
There ain't a lot we had to know
except that I wanted you to be wherever I'd go.

Will anything ever be sweeter than those days?
Nobody's gonna replace all that we shared
    with each other in those days,
back in those sweet L. A. days,
sweet L. A. days.

No one could ever replace
how on a Saturday night
we would jump in your car

and how we'd drive through the night
and maybe not get that far.
There wasn't much we had to learn
except that we knew the road would take us
    through every turn.

Will anything ever be sweeter than those days?
Nobody's gonna replace all that we shared
    with each other in those days,
back in those sweet L. A. days,
sweet L. A. days.

Ooee baby it's takin' me back,
back to those L.A. days,
sweet, sweet, sweet, sweet, sweet, sweet
    L.A. days.
They can't be taken away,
not those L.A. days, no,
those L.A. days, sweet L.A. days.

SWEET L.A. DAYS

Lyric by NEIL DIAMOND

WATER WARS

WHEN PROSPECTORS RUSHED WEST in search of gold in 1849, they marked the beginning of another California obsession—the fight for liquid gold, a.k.a. water. Before the 49ers began using Sierra mountain streams to find and process ore, water was considered an inexhaustible resource covered by "riparian" rights, meaning that whoever owned the land was entitled to a share of the water that passed through it. But as water became more precious, new "appropriative" rights evolved. Applying the "finders, keepers" rule used for gold strikes, miners posted signs appropriating the rights to water they needed, and a system of seniority and constancy of use developed.

Other types of Californian water rights include reserved rights (rights set aside by the federal government), and pueblo rights (city rights to water based on Spanish and Mexican law.) California now has at least six overlapping legal principles that govern water distribution. A large body of case law has established an uneasy hierarchy among them, but confusion and disputes continue to this day.

In California, irrigation has become increasingly vital, as water supply is often found hundreds of miles away from where is it most required. A prime example is the Imperial Valley, a now-fertile region in the Colorado Desert. Though the valley only gets three inches of rain per year, it has one of the longest growing seasons in the United States (over 300 days) and with irrigation can produce two crops a year. In the late 1930s, the 80-mile All-American Canal was built, drawing water from the Colorado River to irrigate approximately one million acres. Today the Imperial Valley is a major source of dates, cotton, grains, and dairy, as well as winter fruits and vegetables consumed in the northern United States.

But since the time of the Gold Rush, water has been coveted by people with conflicting agricultural, domestic, and environmental needs. Between 1919 and 1923, the Hetch Hetchy Valley was dammed and flooded to provide water for San Francisco, turning a picturesque valley within Yosemite National Park into a reservoir. The fierce debate between environmentalists striving to preserve wilderness and those more concerned with best managing its use began.

The most infamous water conflict was the San Fernando Valley land grab and the subsequent "rape" of Owens Valley. At the turn of the century, Los Angeles's expansion was threatened by a shortage of water. A group of civic leaders began to quietly buy up water rights in an undeveloped agricultural valley 200 miles north of where the U.S. Bureau of Reclamation was considering a major irrigation project. The city speculators convinced Los Angelinos to support an aqueduct that would divert the Owens Valley River water to their city. The federal government abandoned their irrigation plans in 1906 and the aqueduct was completed in 1913. Owens Lake is now a dry lakebed, and thousands of acres of agricultural land in Owens Valley are abandoned. The neo-noir film *Chinatown* (1974), starring Jack Nicholson, was loosely based on the land-grab scandal.

And California's water wars rage on. Due to a variety of influences, including environmental movements of the 1960s, '70s, and '80s, cutbacks in federally funded water projects, California's rapid population growth in the late 1980s, and global climate change, California's water rights and water protection issues are becoming more complex. Indeed, as former E.P.A. Chief Christine Witman warned in 2002, it seems water quality and quantity will be "the biggest environmental issue we face in the 21st century."

CALIFORNIA COLORS A SONG

BY CHARLOTTE PERKINS GILMAN

I came from Santa Barbara,
I went to San Jose,
Blue sky above—blue sea beside,
Wild gold along the way—
The lovely lavish blossom gold
Ran wild along the way.

The purple mountains loomed beyond,
The soft hills rolled between,
From crest to crest, like smoke at rest,
The eucalyptus screen
Its careless foliage drifting by
Against that all-enfolding sky
The dusky glimmering green;
With live-oak masses drowsing dark
On the slopes of April green;
More joy than any eye can hold,
Not only blue, not only gold,
But bronze and olive green.

SF 14

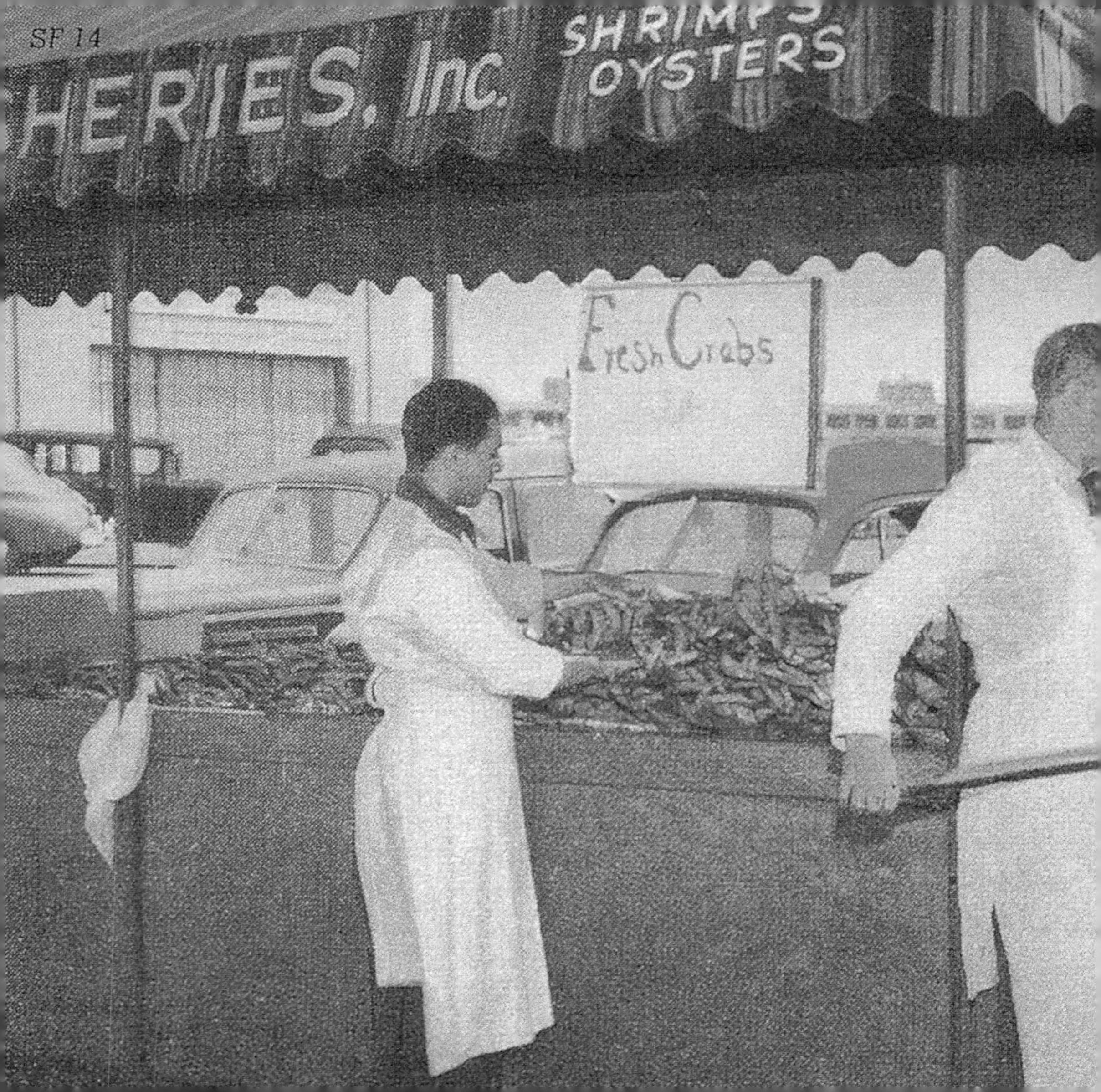

Shrimp and Avocado Salad

A QUINTESSENTIAL CALIFORNIA MEAL, THIS CREATIVE SALAD INCORPORATES FRESH SHRIMP AND CREAMY AVOCADOS, TWO INGREDIENTS READILY AVAILABLE IN THE GOLDEN STATE. AVOCADOS, BROUGHT TO CALIFORNIA FROM MEXICO, HAVE BECOME AN IMPORTANT CASH CROP FOR THE STATE, WHICH PRODUCES 95 PERCENT OF THE AVOCADOS SOLD IN THE UNITED STATES. THE SWEET MANGO AND ZESTY VINAIGRETTE PERFECTLY ACCENT THE PEPPERY ARUGULA AND SALTY SHRIMP, MAKING THIS AN EASY DINNER SALAD TO ENJOY ANY NIGHT OF THE WEEK.

1. Begin by preparing the vinaigrette in a large bowl (you will be tossing the shrimp in later).

2. Whisk all ingredients together and set aside.

3. Combine avocado, mango, and red onion. Dress lightly with vinaigrette. Set aside and begin preparing shrimp.

4. To prepare to shrimp, season with salt and pepper.

5. Heat oil in a heavy skillet over medium-high heat. Add shrimp, garlic, and orange zest.

6. When cooked through (about 3 minutes), remove from heat and add orange juice.

7. Add shrimp, garlic, and orange to vinaigrette. Toss to combine.

8. In another bowl, lightly toss arugula with a few tablespoons of vinaigrette. Lightly salt and pepper and divide onto 4 plates.

9. Mound avocado and mango onto center of each plate and surround with shrimp.

10. Drizzle with dressing and serve warm. (Reserve any additional dressing for later use.)

SERVES 4

VINAIGRETTE:
$^1/_2$ cup olive oil

$^1/_4$ cup raspberry vinegar

1 lime, juiced and zested

1 tablespoon Dijon mustard

1 tablespoon paprika

1 teaspoon sugar

$^1/_4$ cup chopped cilantro

Salt and pepper to taste

SALAD:
2 (loosely packed) cups arugula

1 Haas avocado, peeled, seeded, and diced

1 mango, peeled, seeded, and diced

$^1/_4$ cup red onion, finely chopped

SHRIMP:
20 large shrimp, peeled and deveined

Salt and pepper to taste

1 orange, zested and juiced

1 tablespoon extra-virgin olive oil

3 cloves garlic, minced

THE BIG SCREEN

CLASSICS

***All About Eve* (1950):** A seemingly naive ingénue worms her way into the inner circle of her supposed idol, a talented but aging stage actress.

***Chinatown* (1974):** A 1930s L.A. private detective hired to investigate an adultery case uncovers a plot involving water shortages, land acquisition, bribery, and murder.

***Citizen Kane* (1941):** Orson Wells' landmark film, whose central character is loosely based on William Randolph Hearst, depicts the rise and fall of a wealthy newspaper publisher corrupted and isolated by power.

***East of Eden* (1955):** The black sheep of a pre-World War I truck farming family competes with his brother for his father's love in this modern Cain and Abel story.

***Escape from Alcatraz* (1979):** In this dramatization of a real (and possibly successful) 1962 escape attempt, three men plan and execute an elaborate prison break from a maximum-security penitentiary located on an island in the San Francisco Bay.

COMEDY

Beverly Hills Cop (1984): **When his best friend is murdered, a brash, wisecracking Detroit cop heads to stiff, upscale Beverly Hills to track down the killer.**

Clueless (1995): **In this modern adaptation of Jane Austen's *Emma*, a popular Beverly Hills teen, who enjoys playing matchmaker and making-over friends, discovers that when it comes to her own love life, she's pretty clueless.**

Gidget (1959): **A perky, teenage tomboy spends the summer in Malibu learning about surfing and love from a cool beach bum.**

The Parent Trap (1998): **When identical twins who were separated at birth meet at summer camp, they plot to switch places and reunite their estranged parents.**

The Player (1992): **In this vicious Hollywood satire, a studio executive, threatened by a mysterious writer** he'd rejected, tries to evade the law and keep his job after committing a desperate act.

What's up Doc? (1972): **An absent-minded professor is pursued by a flakey coed dropout as they both become involved in a madcap search for missing jewels, top-secret documents, and igneous rocks.**

DRAMA

Coming Home (1978): **A lonely woman whose hawkish husband is fighting in Vietnam changes her politics and experiences a sexual awakening when she falls for an embittered vet paralyzed in combat.**

Dirty Harry (1971): **A maverick detective with little concern for rules tries to hunt down a sadistic serial killer.**

E.T. the Extra-Terrestrial (1982): **A young boy befriends a stranded alien botanist and helps him return to his home planet.**

The Graduate (1967): A confused, directionless college graduate is seduced by the wife of his father's friend, only to fall in love with the spiteful woman's daughter.

Mommie Dearest (1981): Based on a the life of actress Joan Crawford as seen through the eyes of her adopted children, this film is a searing account of how problems with men, alcohol, and show biz turn the declining star into an abusive mother.

MUSIC & ROMANCE

Almost Famous (2000): A high-school journalist, asked by *Rolling Stone* to cover an up-and-coming band on tour, struggles to maintain his objectivity as he's seduced by the 1970's rock scene.

Harold and Maude (1971): Harold, a young depressive obsessed with death, falls for the vivacious, 79-year-old Maude and finally learns to appreciate life.

Pretty Woman (1990): A corporate raider hires a free-spirited prostitute to be his escort for the week and unexpectedly falls in love.

Pulp Fiction (1994): This film of violence and redemption interweaves multiple storylines involving two hit men and their boss's wife, a down-and-out fighter asked to take a dive, and two lovers who hold up a diner.

Who Framed Roger Rabbit (1988): Animated and live-action characters co-mingle as a cartoon rabbit hires a cartoon-hating detective to investigate alleged infidelities of the rabbit's wife and later prove the rabbit's innocence when he is accused of murder.

HORROR & SUSPENSE

The Birds (1963): A rich female socialite visits a friend in his sleepy coastal town, upsetting his possessive mother and his former lover and seemingly triggering an onslaught of terrifying, chaotic bird attacks.

Invasion of the Body Snatchers (1978): The last four humans left in San Francisco struggle to survive after they discover that people are being replaced with emotionless alien clones.

Pacific Heights (1990): An over-mortgaged couple leases the downstairs level of their dream house to a sociopathic scam artist who's out to claim the house for himself.

Play Misty for Me (1971): When a male disc jockey tries to return to his girlfriend after having a brief fling with a female fan, the fan's obsession takes a frightening and perhaps even deadly turn.

Poltergeist (1982): When poltergeists kidnap a suburban family's daughter and trap her in the spirit world, the family calls in a team of paranormal experts to perform an elaborate exorcism.

Psycho (1960): A young female embezzler makes the unfortunate decision to check into the Bates Motel, an establishment run by a troubled man with terrible secrets.

That limousine in which you made the scene
suits you to a "T"
if all that you want to be
is somebody that don't never walk.

That big chateau where you want to go
in the South of France
gonna end our big romance.
Don't you do it.

Honey, don't leave L.A.
That Riviera's so far away.
Begging you, s'il vous plaît.
They don't know nothing down in St.—Tropez.
Baby, don't you leave L.A.

I heard it said that you had it made
with your movie star.
But oh, how right you are
if that's really 'bout the best you can do.

You moved my soul,
so I played the role
of your backdoor man.
Yes, and now I can't really complain,
'cause I love you.

Honey, don't leave L.A.
That Riviera's so far away.
Begging you, s'il vous plaît.
They don't know nothing down in St.—Tropez.
Mama, don't you leave,
    baby, don't you leave L.A.

HONEY, DON'T
LEAVE L.A.

BY DANNY KORTCHMAR

We have learned the great secret along the way from surf to mountains: you don't have to look busy to be busy. You don't have to scowl and pout and paw the turf and summon ghosts of Jung and séances of Freud to prove yourself an intellectual pomegranate ripe with concepts, creative papa to the world of philosophies, technologies, science, and arts.

—Ray Bradbury

AS EARL ROGERS' DAUGHTER, I had been able to get anyplace I wanted to go....AWE was something I had never felt. My father had taken me to Mr. Hearst to get me a job, and Mr. Hearst had been real great to me....Nevertheless at the thought of this ride alone with him I shook with the worst case of stage fright I was ever to know. In our many years together I was to learn how shy he was with strangers, how much more often he listened than spoke, how kind his responses were, but I did not know this then.

"THE RANCH": HEARST AND SAN SIMEON
BY ADELA ROGERS ST. JOHNS

One thing I had known because his mother, Phoebe Apperson Hearst, had explained it to my grandmother, Adela Andrus Rogers. No one ever quoted Mr. Hearst without mimicking that unique high light voice. The small trumpet squeak of an elephant is a surprise....

He picked me up and we went along quietly beside the Pacific Ocean, in the late afternoon light,... Mr. Hearst far in one corner of the big luxurious limousine, me in the other.

As we swung in from the sea toward Oxnard and the stretch of hills and fruitful valley, we were still silent....So I spoke, "I don't know whether I could be happy away from the sea. I think I got booted out of Bryn Mawr because I couldn't bear to stay away—"

He turned to look at me with a smile. He said, "I never thought of that as an alibi for my getting booted out of Harvard. I thought it was natural villainy...."

On the terrace of one of the white-stucco three-story "cottages" that were the only houses then finished, Mr. Hearst bowed and told me a courteous good night and thanked me for my company.

A maid was waiting in my room, the blaze of a wood fire in the huge fireplace was at the moment more important than art treasures and the light gleaming from behind silken shades, and silver sconces gave the peaceful and comforting effect of candlelight. The maid brought a tray of sandwiches, fruit and cake, milk and hot chocolate, and I thought to myself, This is a life I shall be glad to have known....

The fog had fled before the sun when I woke up, in the daylight the room was the richest and most ornate I had ever seen. Exquisite statuettes, priceless brocade hangings, inlaid furniture, the ceiling had been brought from a palace of Richelieu's, the Renaissance décor was deep and rich in color....

My fire was lighted again, I put on a robe and rang, and asked the maid who came—there was twenty-four-hour service of all kinds—for coffee. With a pleasant smile she said I would have to go up to the Castle for that. This was almost the only thing I found difficult about the Ranch....I once asked Marion Davies about this incongruous bit amid the luxury, the meticulous service, and extravagant indulgence by which guests were surrounded. She said W.R. did not approve of breakfast in bed. If people did not get up and get dressed they might frowst away hours that could better be spent outdoors. He thought, Marion said, that the wonderful walk through morning dew and freshness with the sparkle of the sea below and mountain air blowing from above the Sierras was a good way to start the day. I'm sure it was but at the time I thought I could have appreciated it more with one cup of coffee under my riding britches or my tennis skirt.

On that visit the Castle, La Cuesta Encantada, or Enchanted Hill, was far from completed....For this reason William Randolph Hearst's architect was in residence.

In this setting and company Miss Julia Morgan had to be a double take of unexpectedness. For she was a small, skinny, self-effacing lady whose iron will was fem incognita and sotto voce. Her graying hair was held in a small knob at the back of her head by bone pins, her gray tweed tailored suit was inches too long, and she used no make-up at all....She had designed the unforgettable Tower of Jewels for the 1915 San Francisco World's Fair and she designed and built the Hearst Ranch and everything that had to do with it as long as Mr. Hearst was building it.

As I stood in the window of my own bedroom that morning I said a prayer which I didn't believe in to a God I was convinced didn't exist to the effect that IF there was a heaven to which I would go permanently I hoped it would look like this....

Just then the door opened and to my surprise in came a friend of mine from New York. Helena Young was the wife of a well-known jurist and with her, help us all, was the lady of the Castle. I had never before met Mrs. Hearst and I was astonished at her youth and sparkling handsomeness. She had on a pink Irish linen morning dress, no lady had ever heard of slacks or shorts much less worn them. Mrs. Hearst's hair was dark and worn in an elaborate crown.

Helena bounced as usual, we said the usual things about my trip up, what a lovely morning, then

Helena said, "You know Marion Davies, don't you?"

I said, "Yes, I know her." I thought I might as well fall off a tightrope as choke on my own bated breath, so I said, "Mr. Hearst introduced me to her." I hoped this implied that I hadn't invented Marion Davies. It wasn't me who elevated her to the left hand of the throne. Nevertheless she was my friend, so I said, "I like her a lot."

All right, I thought, I will now be ordered to the Towner and nobody will find me for years. I will probably be beheaded, it seems to me my chances of survival are not very good at this moment.

Helena said reassuringly, "Millicent is just curious."

Mrs. Hearst smiled at me and said, "What does she call him?"

I said, "She calls him W. R."

"And what does he call her?"

"He calls her Marion," and you know at this very moment I can hear him calling, "Mare—eee—on, where's Mare—eee—on?" To the day of his death he wanted to know every minute where she was.

Then we talked about the yacht at the pier below and Mrs. Hearst told me why her husband had given up politics. In the beginning he had thought it was his duty to offer to serve his country in government. Then, he found the people didn't want him. Now, we have the Rockefellers and the Kennedys but when

Mr. Hearst ran for governor we were against great wealth for candidates, we were still committed to the log cabin. So there was no obligation to continue. He wouldn't quit, she said, just because Congress bored him—as everything might except his newspapers. And the Ranch.

Mrs. Hearst said she didn't like the West. Not even the Ranch.

...Just last summer [1965] I went to Southampton to talk to Mrs. Hearst and she said again quite simply that one of the things that had kept her and Mr. Hearst apart so much was that he loved the West, and she was an Easterner. So she kept the Eastern house and estates and apartments going and he stayed at San Simeon. Of all places on earth the spot he loved the best.

On that summer day in the glorious house at Southampton when he had been dead for fifteen years, Mrs. Hearst told me about her first date with young William Randolph Hearst. Even then, this East-West angle came up.

At that time she was Millicent Willson and she and her sister Anita were favorites on the new York musical comedy stage. Not in the chorus as Marion Davies and her sister Rene were—the Willson girls were featured singers and dancers, both had some talent and a lot of beauty. An old-timer told me they had what is called class.

"When he asked me to go out with him," Mrs. Hearst said, "my mother was against it. We were carefully supervised in those days and I recall she said, 'Who is he? Some young fellow from out West somewhere, isn't he?' She insisted Anita had to come or I couldn't go. Well, he took us down to the *Journal*, the *New York Journal*, we'd hardly heard of it, and he showed us over it, all over it. I hadn't the foggiest notion what we were doing, walking miles on rough boards in thin, high-heeled evening slippers, and I thought my feet would kill me. Of course this wasn't our idea of a good time. We wanted to go to Sherry's or Bustanoby's. More than that Anita kept whispering to me, 'We're going to get thrown out of here, Milly, the way he behaves you'd think he owned it.' It wasn't until our next trip that I found out he did—own it, I mean. I told Anita and at first she wouldn't believe me. She said, 'He's like all Westerners. All big brag strutting around as though they owned the earth.' But—" Mrs. Hearst stopped to smile, but whether at me or that long-ago young Westerner talking so big I couldn't tell. "I guess I must have fallen in love with him at once, he asked me to marry him two weeks later and I said yes right away...."

THE SIGHTS

❀ ❀ ❀

Disneyland: The idea for the theme park came from Walt Disney's wish for a new type of amusement park, one that would be clean and would have attractions that parents and children could enjoy together. The amusement park, located in rural Anaheim, south of Los Angeles, cost Disney $17 million and was opened in 1955 with 18 attractions (it now has 60). Since then it has been visited by more than 450 million people. In one year guests buy 4 million hamburgers, 1.6 million hot dogs, 3.4 million orders of French fries, and 1.2 million gallons of soft drinks.

❀ ❀ ❀

Sunset Strip: The best known portion of Sunset Boulevard is the mile-and-a-half stretch of Sunset between Hollywood and Beverly Hills that has been dubbed the "Sunset Strip." It embraces a premier collection of rock clubs, hotels, restaurants, boutiques, and Hollywood nightclubs that are on the cutting edge of the entertainment business. Highlights of the strip include the Chateau Marmont Hotel (where Natalie Wood and James Dean first met), the House of Blues (co-owned by Dan Akroyd), The Sky Bar at the Mondrian Hotel, the Tower Records flagship store, the original Spago Restaurant (birthplace of California Cuisine), the Comedy Store (where David Letterman, Jim Carrey, and Michael Keaton got their starts), and the Viper Room (where actor River Phoenix died in 1993).

❀ ❀ ❀

Seventeen-Mile Drive: One of the prettiest tours in California, it costs $8.00 to enter the area, but it is well worth the money. The route gets its name because the whole trip is 17 miles around in a circle. There are three entrances: from Pacific Grove, Carmel, or Highway 1. Part of the drive is by the ocean, while the rest is canopied by trees and multimillion-dollar fairy-tale homes. As the winding road approaches the coast, turbulent surf, twisted cypress trees, and herds of sunbathing sea lions come into view. Cypress Point, a scenic overlook with spectacular views, is the best vantage point from which to view the seals (who in the spring come ashore to have their pups here). The drive is also home to some of the best golf courses in California, if not the world, among them Pebble Beach, Spyglass, Cypress Point, and the Links at Spanish Bay.

❈ ❈ ❈

Route 66: Twenty-four hundred miles in length, this historic trail travels from east to west through eight states: Illinois, Missouri, Kansas, Oklahoma, Texas, New Mexico, Arizona, and California. The California stretch covers 320 miles from Needles to Santa Monica. Two hundred and fourteen of those miles lead through the Mojave Desert. Where Route 66 ends in Santa Monica, a plaque states simply "Will Rogers Highway, dedicated 1952 to Will Rogers, Humorist, World Traveler, Good Neighbor. This Main Street of America, Highway 66 was the first road he traveled in a career that led him straight to the hearts of his countrymen."

❈ ❈ ❈

J. Paul Getty Museum: In a city full of world-class museums, the new Getty, on 750 acres in the Santa Monica Mountain foothills, designed by Richard Meier and completed in 1997, is more than just a place to view art. It is an architectural wonder, a collection of special gardens, a research institute, and an extraordinary vista point. J. Paul Getty, who made his billions in Standard Oil, left $1.2 billion to the Getty Trust—an amount which has now grown to more than $5 billion—to build a museum to house his art collection. The parking area is at the bottom of the hill, and a tram whisks visitors to the museum at the top, physically transporting them from everyday routine up to a kingdom of dreams.

Big Sur: The name for this 90-mile stretch of coast south of San Francisco derives from the original Spanish-language El Sur Grande, which translates as "the Big South." Its most northern end is at Carmel, and it ends at San Simeon, which is about 240 road miles north of Los Angeles. Ever since the early Monterey settlers arrived, Big Sur has been known throughout the world as the prettiest—and most treacherous—drive along the California coast. It is a region that remains largely undeveloped to this day.

Squaw Valley: The 1960 Winter Olympic Games at Squaw Valley was home to a lot of firsts: the first ever winter Olympics held in the western United States and the first to be televised; the first games where computers were used to tabulate results; the first and only time in modern Olympic history all the athletes were housed under one roof (in the Olympic Village Inn, built for the occasion); and in a historic Cold War face-off, the first time the American hockey team defeated the Russians in a heart pounding, down- to-the-wire, 3-2 semifinal victory.

Lake Tahoe: Located about two hours northeast of San Francisco, the lake was formed by geologic-block faulting about 2 to 3 million years ago. At 1,645 feet, it is the second deepest lake in the United States and the tenth deepest in the world. The amount of water that evaporates from the surface of Lake Tahoe every year could supply a city the size of Los Angeles for five years. Truly enormous (191 square miles) and regally beautiful, Lake Tahoe is a hot spot for tourists and sports enthusiasts year round. In the winter, skiers and snow boarders flock to the area to enjoy some of the best powder in California.

San Diego Zoo: The history of the Zoo began when foreign animals brought for the 1915 Panama-California International Exposition inspired Dr. Harry Wegeforth to open a zoo. Known for its ongoing conservation efforts, the San Diego Zoo today boasts over 220 species of mammals, 1450 species of birds, and 166 species of reptiles—many of which are endangered species. Some of the rarest finds include the Szechuan takin (the last forest musk ox), Mhor's gazelle (extinct in the wild), the delightful Bornean bearded pig, the tiny Kazakhastan corsac fox, the sun bear, the endangered lion-tailed macaques, spectacled bears, Malayan tapirs, koalas, Guam rails (extinct in the wild), the Tahiti blue lorry (one of the rarest parrots in the world), dusky padmelons, Nubian soemmering's gazelle, and Tasmanian devils. But the Zoo is perhaps most famous for the Giant Pandas it has been able to breed in captivity.

❀ ❀ ❀

Coit Tower: Located on San Francisco's Telegraph Hill, Coit Tower has provided visitors and locals alike with impressive views since its completion in 1933. Lillie Hitchcock Coit, philanthropist and admirer of the fire fighters at the 1906 earthquake fire, left funds to the city for beautification of San Francisco. The funds were used to construct the 210-foot-tall Art Deco tower in 1933. Its design was quite controversial at the time. Works Progress Administration murals, inspired by Diego Rivera and now protected as a historical treasure, can be viewed inside the first floor of Coit Tower.

❈ ❈ ❈

Catalina Island: Although people have been living on this island 25 miles off the coast of Los Angeles for over 7,000 years, it was William Wrigley Jr., self-made chewing-gum king, who made it famous. World War I hit some industries hard, but chewing gum thrived. Not only was Wrigley able to take over the Chicago Cubs, but in 1919 he purchased Catalina, sight unseen, for $3 million. The Cubs and Catalina became Wrigley's twin passions, and by spring of 1921 he arranged their union: The ball club would train on the island. With sportswriters sending dispatches back to frigid Chicago chronicling the Cubbies island frolics, Catalina became the new vacation hotspot. Wrigley only owned the Cubs for 16 years, but until 1951 they continued traveling west for spring training on the "Isle with a Smile."

❈ ❈ ❈

Hearst Castle: William Randolph Hearst built "La Cuesta Encantada" on 40,000 acres of ranchland his father had purchased near San Simeon in 1865. Construction began in 1919 and was not completed until 1947. The magnificent main house, "Casa Grande," has 38 bedrooms and 41 bathrooms. The indoor Roman pool is designed with gold-trimmed tile and is modeled after the baths at Caracalla. Although such extravagance is common among celebrities today, in the 1940s, after WWII, Hearst was criticized for his lavish home. Orson Welles based the fictional Xanadu on Hearst's castle in his cult-classic film *Citizen Kane*. Hearst died in 1951, and his home is now open to the public.

NOVEMBER SURF

BY ROBINSON JEFFERS

Some lucky day each November great waves awake and are drawn
Like smoking mountains bright from the west
And come and cover the cliff with white violent cleanness: then suddenly
The old granite forgets half a year's filth:
The orange-peel, eggshells, papers, pieces of clothing, the clots
Of dung in corners of the rock, and used
Sheaths that make light love safe in the evenings: all the droppings of the
    summer
Idlers washed off in a winter ecstasy:
I think this cumbered continent envies its cliff then....But all seasons
The earth, in her childlike prophetic sleep,
Keeps dreaming of the bath of a storm that prepares up the long coast
Of the future to scour more than her sea-lines:
The cities gone down, the people fewer and the hawks more numerous,
The rivers mouth to source pure; when the two-footed
Mammal, being someways one of the nobler animals, regains
The dignity of room, the value of rareness.

Fish Tacos

12 fresh cod fillets

12 corn tortillas

1 head cabbage, shredded

6 limes, quartered

FRESH, MILD WHITE FISH FRIED TO CRISPY PERFECTION, CABBAGE, AND SALSA ALL WRAPPED IN A TORTILLA MAKE UP THE FISH TACO, A SOUTHERN CALIFORNIA STAPLE. FISH TACOS WERE MADE POPULAR ON THE BAJA PENINSULA WHERE THE SEAFOOD IS FRESH AND ABUNDANT, AND THEY CAN BE DRESSED UP WITH TOMATO OR CHILI SALSAS, OR ENJOYED SIMPLY WRAPPED IN A HOT WHEAT TORTILLA. ANY MILD WHITE FISH WILL WORK IN THIS RECIPE, JUST BE SURE TO GET THE FRESHEST FISH FOR THE BEST TASTE.

WHITE SAUCE:

$1/2$ cup mayonnaise

$1/2$ cup plain yogurt

2 tablespoons cilantro, chopped

BEER BATTER:

1 cup flour

1 cup dark beer

$1/2$ tablespoon garlic salt

Pepper to taste

1. Begin by cleaning fish in a large bowl of cold, salted water. Pat fish dry and dice into 1- to 2-inch cubes.

2. In a small serving bowl, combine mayonnaise, yogurt, and cilantro. Place in refrigerator to chill.

3. In another serving bowl, combine tomatoes, garlic, onion, cilantro, lime juice, and jalapeno. Add salt and pepper to taste. Set aside.

4. In a small skillet, lightly warm tortillas.

5. In a large, heavy skillet or deep-fat fryer, place enough vegetable oil to completely submerge fish pieces. Heat oil to 375 °F.

6. Combine flour, beer, and spices, stirring until well incorporated.

7. Dunk fish cubes into batter and fry in a single layer, turning as needed to achieve a uniform golden-brown crispiness. Repeat until all the fish is cooked.

8. Lightly sprinkle with salt and lime juice as fish comes out.

   Assemble each taco by layering a warm tortilla with white sauce, shredded cabbage, several fish cubes, and pico de gallo.

9. Serve with limes and hot sauce.

SERVES 6

PICO DE GALLO:

6 tomatoes, diced

2 cloves garlic, minced

¹/₂ onion, diced

2 tablespoons cilantro, chopped

Juice of 1 lime

2 jalapeno peppers, seeded and chopped (It is best to use rubber gloves when handling hot peppers. If you choose not to use gloves, please exercise caution.)

Salt and pepper to taste

Vegetable oil for frying

Lime juice

Salt

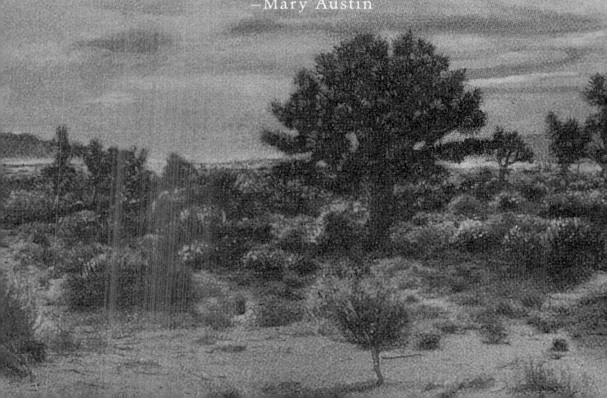

For all the toll the desert takes of a man it gives compensations, deep breaths, deep sleep, and the communion of the stars.

—Mary Austin

FROM THE VALLEY OF THE MOON
BY JACK LONDON

South they held along the coast, hunting, fishing, swimming, and horse-buying. Billy shipped his purchases on the coasting steamers. Through Del Norte and Humboldt counties they went, and through Mendocino into Sonoma—counties larger than Eastern states—threading the giant woods, whipping innumerable trout streams, and crossing countless rich valleys. Ever Saxon sought the valley of the moon. Sometimes, when all seemed fair, the lack was a railroad, sometimes madroño and manzanita trees, and, usually, there was too much fog.

"We do want a sun-cocktail once in a while," she told Billy.

"Yep," was his answer. "Too much fog might make us soggy. What we're after is betwixt an' between, an' we'll have to get back from the coast a ways to find it."

This was in the fall of the year, and they turned their backs on the Pacific at old Fort Ross and entered the Russian River Valley, far below Ukiah, by way of Cazadero and Guerneville. At Santa Rosa Billy was delayed with the shipping of several horses, so that it was not until afternoon that he drove south and east for Sonoma Valley.

Rising from rolling stubble fields, Bennett Peak towered hot in the sun, a row of bastion hills leaning against its base. But hills and mountains on that side showed bare and heated, though beautiful with the sunburnt tawniness of California.

"The turn to the right will take you to Glen Ellen, too, only it's longer and steeper grades. But your mares don't look as though it'd bother them."

"Which is the prettiest way?" Saxon asked.

"Oh, the right-hand road, by all means," said the man. "That's Sonoma Mountain there, and the road skirts it pretty well up, and goes through Cooper's Grove."

Billy did not start immediately after they had said good-bye, and he and Saxon, heads over shoulders, watched the roused Barbarossa plunging mutinously on toward Santa Rosa.

"Gee!" Billy said. "I'd like to be up there next spring."

At the crossroads Billy hesitated and looked at Saxon.

"What if it is longer?" she said. "Look how beautiful it is—all covered with green woods; and I just know those are redwoods in the canyons. You never can tell. The valley of the moon might be right up there somewhere. And it would never do to miss it just in order to save half an hour."

They took the turn to the right and began crossing a series of steep foothills. As they approached the mountain there were signs of a greater abundance of water. They drove beside a running stream, and, though the vineyards on the hills were summer-dry, the farmhouses in the hollows and on the levels were grouped about with splendid trees.

"Maybe it sounds funny," Saxon observed; "but I'm beginning to love that mountain already. It almost seems as if I'd seen it before, somehow, it's so all-around satisfying—oh!"

Crossing a bridge and rounding a sharp turn, they were suddenly enveloped in a mysterious coolness and gloom. All about them arose stately trunks of redwood. The forest floor was a rosy carpet of autumn fronds. Occasional shafts of sunlight, penetrating the deep shade, warmed the somberness of the grove. Alluring paths led off among the trees and into cozy nooks made by circles of red columns growing around the dust of vanished ancestors—witnessing the titanic dimensions of those ancestors by the girth of the circles in which they stood.

Out of the grove they pulled to the steep divide, which was no more than a buttress of Sonoma Mountain. The way led on through rolling upland and across small dips and canyons, all well wooded and a-drip with water. In places the road was muddy from wayside springs.

"The mountain's a sponge," said Billy. "Here it is, the tail end of dry summer, an' the ground's just leakin' everywhere."

"I know I've never been here before," Saxon communed aloud. "But it's all so familiar! So I must have dreamed it. And there's madroño!—a whole grove! And manzanita! Why, I feel just as if I was coming home [...] Oh, Billy, if it should turn out to be over valley."

"Plastered against the side of a mountain?" he queried, with a skeptical laugh.

"No; I don't mean that. I mean on the way to our valley. Because the way—all ways—to our valley must be beautiful. And this; I've seen it all before, dreamed it."

"It's great," he said sympathetically. "I wouldn't trade a square mile of this kind of country for the whole Sacramento Valley, with the river islands thrown in and Middle River for good measure. If they ain't deer up there, I miss my guess. An' where they's springs they's streams, an' streams means trout."

They passed a large and comfortable farmhouse, surrounded by wandering barns and cow-sheds, went on under forest arches, and emerged beside a field with which Saxon was instantly enchanted. It flowed in a gentle concave from the road up the mountain, its farther boundary an unbroken line of timber. The field glowed like rough gold in the approaching sunset, and near the middle of it stood a solitary great redwood, with blasted top suggesting a nesting aerie for eagles. The timber beyond clothed the mountain in solid green to what they took to be the top. But, as they drove on, Saxon, looking back upon what she called her field, saw the real summit of Sonoma towering beyond, the mountain behind her field a mere spur upon the side of the larger mass.

Ahead and toward the right, across sheer ridges of the mountains, separated by deep green canyons and broadening lower down into rolling orchards and vineyards, they caught their first sight of Sonoma Valley and the wild mountains that rimmed its eastern side. To the left they gazed across a golden land of small hills and valleys. Beyond, to the north, they glimpsed another portion of the valley, and, still beyond, the opposing wall of the valley—a range of mountains, the highest of which reared its red and battered ancient crater against a rosy and mellowing sky. From north to southeast, the mountain rim curved in the brightness of the sun, while Saxon and Billy were already in the shadow of evening. He looked at Saxon, noted the ravished ecstasy of her face, and stopped the horses. All the western sky was blushing to rose, which descended upon the mountains, touching them with wine and ruby. Sonoma Valley began to fill with a purple flood, laving the mountain bases, rising, inundating, drowning them in its purple. Saxon pointed in silence, indicating that the purple flood was the sunset shadow of Sonoma Mountain. Billy nodded, then chirruped to the mares, and the descent began through a warm and colorful twilight.

On the elevated sections of the road they felt the cool, delicious breeze from the Pacific forty miles away; while from each little dip and hollow came warm breaths of autumn earth, spicy with sunburnt grass and fallen leaves and passing flowers.

They came to the rim of a deep canyon that seemed to penetrate to the heart of Sonoma Mountain. Again, with no word spoken, merely from watching Saxon, Billy stopped the wagon. The canyon was wildly beautiful. Tall redwoods lined its entire length. On its farther rim stood three rugged knolls covered with dense woods of spruce and oak. From between the knolls, a feeder to the main canyon and likewise fringed with redwoods, emerged a smaller canyon. Billy pointed to a stubble field that lay at the feet of the knolls.

"It's in fields like that I've seen my mares a-pasturing," he said.

They dropped down into the canyon, the road following a stream

that sang under maples and alders. The sunset fires, refracted from the cloud-driftage of the autumn sky, bathed the canyons with crimson, in which ruddy-limbed madroños and wine-wooded manzanitas burnt and smoldered. The air was aromatic with laurel. Wild grapevines bridged the stream from tree to tree. Oaks of many sorts were veiled in lacy Spanish moss. Ferns and brakes grew lush beside the stream. From somewhere came the plaint of a mourning dove. Fifty feet above the ground, almost over their heads, a Douglas squirrel crossed the road—a flash of gray between two trees; and they marked the continuance of its aerial passage by the bending of the boughs.

"I've got a hunch," said Billy.

"Let me say it first," Saxon begged.

He waited, his eyes on her face as she gazed about her in rapture.

"We've found our valley," she whispered. "Was that it?"

More leaping tree squirrels, more ruddy madroños and majestic oaks, more fairy circles of redwoods, and, still beside the singing stream, they passed a gate by the roadside. Before it stood a rural mailbox, on which was lettered "Edmund Hale." Standing under the rustic arch, leaning upon the gate, a man and woman composed a picture so arresting and beautiful that Saxon caught her breath. They were side by side, the delicate hand of the woman curled in the hand of the man, which looked as if made to confer benedictions. His face bore out this impression—a beautiful-browed countenance, with large, benevolent gray eyes under a wealth of white hair that shone like spun glass. He was fair and large; the little woman beside him was daintily wrought. She was saffron-brown, as a woman of the white race can well be, with smiling eyes of bluest blue. In quaint sage-green draperies, she seemed a flower, with her small vivid face irresistibly reminding Saxon of a springtime wake-robin.

Perhaps the picture made by Saxon and Billy was equally arresting and beautiful, as they drove down through the golden end of day. The two couples had eyes only for each other. The little woman beamed joyously. The man's face glowed into the benediction that had trembled there. To Saxon, like the field up the mountain, like the mountain itself, it seemed that she had always known this adorable pair. She knew that she loved them.

"How d'ye do," said Billy.

"You blessed children," said the man. "I wonder if you know how dear you look sitting there."

That was all. The wagon had passed by, rustling down the road, which was carpeted with fallen leaves of maple, oak, and alder. Then they came to the meeting of the two creeks.

"Oh, what a place for a home," Saxon cried, pointing across Wild Water. "See, Billy; on that bench there above the meadow."

"It's a rich bottom, Saxon; and so is the bench rich. Look at the big trees on it. An' they's sure to be springs."

"Drive over," she said.

Forsaking the main road, they crossed Wild Water on a narrow bridge and continued along an ancient, rutted road that ran beside an

191

equally ancient worm-fence of split redwood rails. They came to a gate, open and off its hinges, through which the road led out on the bench.

"This is it—I know it," Saxon said with conviction. "Drive in, Billy."

A small, whitewashed farmhouse with broken windows showed through the trees.

"Talk about your madroños—"

Billy pointed to the father of all madroños, six feet in diameter at its base, sturdy and sound, which stood before the house.

They spoke in low tones as they passed around the house under great oak trees and came to a stop before a small barn. They did not wait to unharness. Tying the horses, they started to explore. The pitch from the bench to the meadow was steep yet thickly wooded with oaks and manzanita. As they crashed through the underbrush they startled a score of quail into flight.

"How about game?" Saxon queried.

Billy grinned, and fell to examining a spring which bubbled a clear stream into the meadow. Here the ground was sunbaked and wide open in a multitude of cracks.

Disappointment leaped into Saxon's face, but Billy, crumbling a clod between his fingers, had not made up his mind.

"It's rich," he pronounced; "—the cream of the soil that's ben washin' down from the hills for ten thousan' years. But—"

He broke off, stared all about, studying the configuration of the meadow, crossed it to the redwood trees beyond, then came back.

"It's no good as is," he said. "But it's the best ever if it's handled right. All it needs is a little common sense an' a lot of drainage. This meadow's a natural basin not yet filled level. They's a sharp slope through the redwoods to the creek. Come on, I'll show you."

They went through the redwoods and came out on Sonoma Creek. At this spot was no singing. The stream poured into a quiet pool. The willows on their side brushed the water. The opposite side was a steep bank. Billy measured the height of the bank with his eye, the depth of the water with a driftwood pole.

"Fifteen feet," he announced. "That allows all kinds of high-divin' from the bank. An' it's a hundred yards of a swim up an' down."

They followed down the pool. It emptied in a riffle, a cross exposed bedrock, into another pool. As they looked, a trout flashed into the air and back, leaving a widening ripple on the quiet surface.

"I guess we won't winter in Carmel," Billy said. "This place was specially manufactured for us. In the morning I'll find out who owns it."

Half an hour later, feeding the horses, he called Saxon's attention to a locomotive whistle.

"You've got your railroad," he said. "That's a train pulling into Glen Ellen, an' it's only a mile from here."

Saxon was dozing off to sleep under the blankets when Billy aroused her.

"Suppose the guy that owns it won't sell?"

"There isn't the slightest doubt," Saxon answered with unruffled certainty. "This is our place. I know it."

WINE COUNTRY

Father Junipero Serra, a Franciscan priest and Spanish missionary, introduced wine grapes to California in the 1760's. He planted a varietal at each of his missions that was descended from the Sardinian vines brought to North America by the Conquistadors.

The mysterious Hungarian count, Ágoston Haraszthy is considered the "Father of the California Wine Industry." He founded the Buena Vista winery in 1855, introduced the use of European vines, and returned to Europe to bring back another 1,400 varieties of grapes to northern California for cultivation.

❈ ❈ ❈

In 1873, a worldwide outbreak of phylloxera, an aphid-like root parasite, decimated the French and American wine industries. A disease-resistant rootstock was ultimately developed in California, and used to reestablish the state's wine industry, but phyllooooxera still exists in the valley today.

❈ ❈ ❈

When Prohibition began in 1919, there were over 600 wineries in Napa and Sonoma Valleys. When it ended in 1933, there were fewer than 50 wineries left that had been permitted to produce "sacramental" wines.

❈ ❈ ❈

Wine production soared during Prohibition because of a loophole in the law that allowed individuals to produce 200 gallons of wine a year for home use. In 1930, more than 150 million gallons of wine were produced in hundreds of thousands of homes. In fact, grapes were in such demand during early Prohibition that prices skyrocketed to levels not seen again until the late 1960s.

❈ ❈ ❈

Napa and Sonoma Valleys' wine industry contribute an estimated $3 billion to the local economy, which is 18% of the county's contribution to the gross domestic product (GDP).

❈ ❈ ❈

Tannins, found in red wine, come from grape skins, seeds, stems, and oak barrels. They help a wine age and develop its distinctive flavor.

❈ ❈ ❈

Thinking of starting your own Napa winery? Break out the checkbook and consider these stats: One acre of unplanted land in wine country can cost from $10,000 to $40,000 and grape presses start at $100,000.

❈ ❈ ❈

Chardonnay and pinot noir varietals thrive in the coastal areas of wine country while the northern inland areas are best for growing cabernet, sauvignon blanc, and merlot.

California produces over 90% of American wines—about 3.3 million tons of grapes are crushed annually to create them.

❈ ❈ ❈

The largest per capita wine consumption of bottles priced over $15 comes from the area stretching between San Diego, California, and Vancouver, British Columbia.

❈ ❈ ❈

Ever wonder why the host gets the first sip? The traditions dates back to times when it was necessary to show the wine was not only drinkable, but also poison-free!

❈ ❈ ❈

Did you know that 98% of all wine in the world is consumed within a week of purchase? So much for stocking the wine cellar!

❈ ❈ ❈

The wine cellars of Beringer Vineyards, the oldest continuously operating winery in Napa, are hand-chiseled rock tunnels carved by Chinese workers returning to the Bay Area after building of the Trans-Continental Railroad. The tunnels maintain a constant temperature of 58°F, perfect for aging wine.

❈ ❈ ❈

An unexpected find in Napa is Jade Lake, a perfectly maintained Chinese-style garden and pagoda found on the grounds of the Chateau Montelena winery. The gardens were created in the 1950s by Yort Wing Frank, a Chinese electrical engineer and owner of the winery at the time. He wanted to enhance the estate with gardens that reminded him of his homeland, and he named the lake after his wife.

※ ※ ※

Wine Country is home to some of the most renowned restaurants in California, no doubt because of their proximity to award-winning vineyards and abundant harvests. One of the most respected is French Laundry owned by Thomas Keller, which has earned a prestigious 3-star rating from the Michelin restaurant guide.

※ ※ ※

For a unique, leisurely and delicious way to tour Napa Valley, take a ride on the historic Napa Valley Wine Train. Enjoy wine tastings and gourmet meals along the 21-mile ride through the picturesque vineyards while relaxing in perfectly restored Pullman cars dating back to the turn of the 20th century.

※ ※ ※

Calistoga is home to an American icon, Old Faithful. This ancient geyser erupts with astounding regularity, amazing onlookers with a towering spray of boiling water every 30 minutes or so. Because of all the springs that can be found in Calistoga, the town has been frequented by tourists seeking the healing effects of the hot water rich in minerals since the mid 1800s.

※ ※ ※

Spring Mountain Vineyard was the setting for the popular '80s prime-time soap "Falcon Crest." The Vineyard's Miravalle estate was home to the ruthless winemaking Channing family, whose matriarch was played by Ronald Reagan's ex—Jane Wyman.

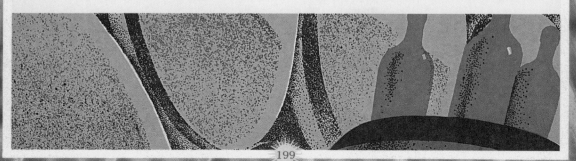

ONE OF THE MOST IMPORTANT Latino activists in U.S. history, Cesar Chavez gained worldwide renown organizing and championing migrant workers in California. Cesar was born on March 31, 1927 near Yuma, Arizona to Librado and Juana Chavez, owners of a small family ranch and country store. In the 1930s, due to hardships of the Great Depression and years of drought, the Chavez family lost both their farm and store. Cesar was 10 years old when the family moved west looking for work.

CESAR CHAVEZ -
VIVA LA CAUSA!

In California, the Chavez family joined the migrant worker community, traveling from farm to farm to harvest fruits and vegetables. For many tough years, the family slept by the roadside or lived in numerous migrant camps. Cesar attended over 35 different schools, often facing harsh discrimination, before finally quitting school after eighth grade to work full-time in the vineyards. In 1948, following a two-year stint in the Navy, he married Helen Fabela. The couple eventually moved to San Jose, where they started their family. At that time, Chavez began studying the writings of St. Francis and Mahatma Gandhi and non-violent means of effecting positive change.

Chavez was recruited in 1952 by the Community Service Organization (CSO), a group that helped Mexicans and Mexican-Americans with issues such as immigration, tax problems, and discrimination. He traveled throughout California encouraging Mexican-Americans to register to vote and quickly developed into a gifted organizer. Chavez became the CSO's general director and held the position from 1958 until 1962, when he resigned to concentrate on organizing farmworkers. His new group, the National Farmworkers Association (NFWA), was later renamed the United Farmworkers (UFW).

In 1965, Chavez and the NFWA led California grape-pickers in a strike demanding higher wages. The strike lasted five years and mobilized over 13 million Americans to show their support by boycotting table grapes. During the strike, Chavez showed his own commitment to what became know as *La Causa* (the cause) and to nonviolent protest by leading a 300-mile pilgrimage walk and by fasting for 25 days. As he finally broke his fast, he was visited by Senator Robert Kennedy, who called Chavez "one of the heroic figures of our time." The strike ended in 1970 when grape growers finally agreed to sign three-year contracts.

But in the late 1960s, the Teamsters had begun fighting to organize farmworkers and strip power from the UFW. When grape growers signed with the Teamsters in 1973, massive UFW strikes spread throughout California, leaving thousands arrested and two dead. The two organizations finally signed a 1977 pact that gave the UFW exclusive rights to organize field workers. The UFW expanded to include all vegetable pickers, and, in 1972, became a member union of the American Federation of Labor and Congress of Industrial Organizations (AFL-CIO).

In the 1980s, Cesar lead a strike and boycott to protest toxic pesticides used on grapes, at one point fasting for 38 days. Cesar Chavez died on April 23, 1993 in Yuma, Arizona at the age of 66. Over 40,000 people attended his funeral. Though his effectiveness in his later years has been disputed, Cesar remains greatly revered as an American labor organizer and an inspirational Latino icon. In 1994, Cesar was posthumously awarded the nation's highest civilian honor, the Presidential Medal of Freedom, by President Clinton. Cesar's UFW organization continues to fight in the fields for improved conditions and higher wages, invoking one of his most famous slogans, *Si, Se Puede!* (Yes, we can!)

FROM PRAYERS FOR A THOUSAND YEARS...

BY JACK KORNFIELD

My simple prayer is that in all things
I learn to love well.
That I learn to touch the ever-changing seasons of life with a
   great heart of compassion.
That I live with the peace and justice I wish for the earth.
That I learn to care fully and let go gracefully.
That I enjoy the abundance of the earth and return to it from
   the natural generosity that is our human birthright.
That through my own life. Through joy and sorrow in thought,
   word, and deed,
I bring benefit and blessings to all that lives.
That my heart and the hearts of all beings learn to be free.

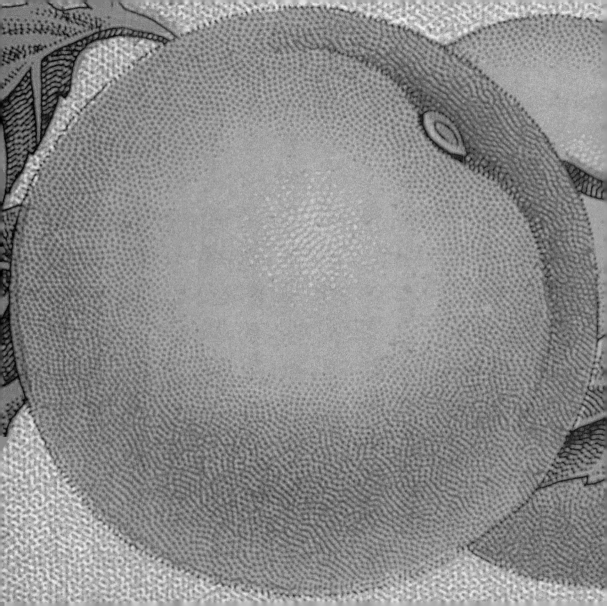

Fresh Apricot Sorbet

Originating in China, apricots traveled across the Persian Empire to Spain where they flourished. From there, Spanish conquistadors brought them to the New World where they were widely grown in the California missions. Today, 95 percent of U.S. apricots are grown in California, and this abundant fruit is wildly popular as a dessert ingredient. This cool and healthy sorbet is the perfect dessert for a California summer night. Serve it after the Shrimp and Avocado Salad for a sweet and light ending to your meal.

1 pound fresh apricots, washed and pitted *

1 lemon, juiced and zested

1/2 cup sugar

1. In a food processor, puree apricots.

2. Add lemon juice and sugar. Pulse several times to combine.

3. Strain mixture into a large bowl and mix in lemon zest.

IF YOU HAVE AN ICE CREAM MAKER:
Refrigerate mixture for 1 hour.

4. Pour into an ice cream maker and freeze according to manufacturer's instructions.

5. Transfer sorbet to an airtight container and freeze for two hours or overnight before serving.

IF YOU DO NOT HAVE AN ICE CREAM MAKER:
4b. Pour sorbet mixture directly from the food processor into a shallow baking pan and place in freezer.

5b. Freeze until firm, stirring every 30 minutes for 2 hours.

6b. Place frozen mixture back in food processor and process until smooth. Return to an airtight container and freeze for 2 hours or overnight before serving.

Serves 4

*If fresh apricots are not available, instead combine 1/2 cup water, 1/4 cup sugar, and 3 cups dried apricots in a saucepan. Bring to a boil, stirring until sugar dissolves, and then remove from heat and let stand until apricots have softened (about 1 hour). Puree apricots and water. Resume with step 2, adding extract as well.

I always want to go north. North up the coast, the destination doesn't matter—Santa Barbara, Cambria, Palo Alto, San Francisco. What matters is the chilly air and ocean light, the promise of the unknown steadily uncoiling as you skim the edge of the continent.

—April Smith

IN THE EARLY MONTHS of World War II, San Francisco's Fillmore district, or the Western Addition, experienced a visible revolution. On the surface it appeared to be totally peaceful and almost a refutation of the term "revolution." The Yakamoto Sea Food Market quietly became Sammy's Shoe Shine Parlor and Smoke Shop. Yashigira's Hardware metamorphosed into La Salon de Beauté owned by Miss Clorinda Jackson. The Japanese shops which sold products to Nisei customers were taken over by enterprising

FROM **I KNOW WHY THE CAGED BIRD SINGS**

BY MAYA ANGELOU

Negro businessmen, and in less than a year became permanent homes away from home for the newly arrived Southern Blacks. Where the odors of tempura, raw fish and *cha* had dominated, the aroma of chitlings, greens and ham hocks now prevailed.

The Asian population dwindled before my eyes. I was unable to tell the Japanese from the Chinese and as yet found no real difference in the national origin of such sounds as Ching and Chan or Moto and Kano.

As the Japanese disappeared, soundlessly and without protest, the Negroes entered with their loud jukeboxes, their just-released animosities and the relief of escape from Southern bonds. The Japanese area became San Francisco's Harlem in a matter of months.

A person unaware of all the factors that make up oppression might have expected sympathy or even support from the Negro newcomers for the dislodged Japanese. Especially in view of the fact that they (the Blacks) had themselves undergone concentration-camp living for centuries in slavery's plantations and later in sharecroppers' cabins. But the sensations of common relationship were missing.

The Black newcomer had been recruited on the desiccated farm lands of Georgia and Mississippi by war-plant labor scouts. The chance to live in two- or three-story apartment buildings (which became instant slums), and to earn two- and even three-figured weekly checks, was blinding. For the first time he could think of himself as a Boss, a Spender. He was able to pay other people to work for him, i.e. the dry cleaners, taxi drivers, waitresses, etc. The shipyards and ammunition plants brought to booming life by the war let him know that he was needed and even appreciated. A completely alien yet very pleasant position for him to experience. Who could expect this man to share his new and dizzying importance with concern for a race that he had never known to exist?

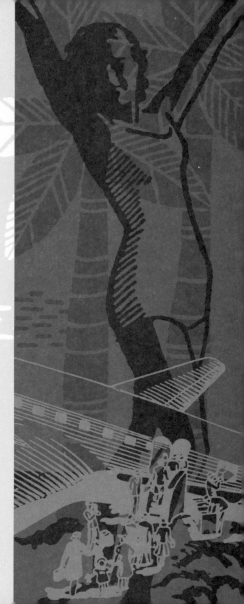

Another reason for his indifference to the Japanese removal was more subtle but was more profoundly felt. The Japanese were not whitefolks. Their eyes, language, and customs belied the white skin and proved to their dark successors that since they didn't have to be feared, neither did they have to be considered. All this was decided unconsciously.

No member of my family and none of the family friends ever mentioned the absent Japanese. It was as if they had never owned or lived in the houses we inhabited. On Post Street, where our house was, the hill skidded slowly down to Fillmore, the market heart of our district. In the two short blocks before it reached its destination, the street housed two day-and-night restaurants, two pool halls, four Chinese restaurants, two gambling houses, plus diners, shoeshine shops, beauty salons, barber shops and at least four churches. To fully grasp the never-ending activity in San Francisco's Negro neighborhood during the war, one need only know that the two blocks described were side streets that were duplicated many times over in the eight- to ten-square-block area.

The air of collective displacement, the imperma-nence of life in wartime and the gauche personalities of the more recent arrivals tended to dissipate my own sense of not belonging. In San Francisco, for the first time, I perceived myself as part of something. Not that I identified with the newcomers, nor with the rare Black descendants of native San Franciscans, nor with the whites or even the Asians, but rather with the times and the city. I understood the arrogance of the young sailors who marched the streets in marauding gangs, approaching every girl as if she were at best a prostitute and at worst an Axis agent bent on making the U.S.A. lose the war. The undertone of fear that San Francisco would be bombed, which was abetted by weekly air-raid warnings and civil defense drills in school, heightened my sense of belonging. Hadn't I, always, but ever and ever, thought that life was just one great risk for the living?

Then the city acted in wartime like an intelligent woman under siege. She gave what she couldn't with safety withhold, and secured those things which lay in her reach. The city became for me the ideal of what I wanted to be as a grownup. Friendly but never gushing, cool but not frigid or distant, distinguished without the awful stiffness.

To San Franciscans "the City That Knows How" was the Bay, the fog, Sir Francis Drake Hotel, Top o' the Mark, Chinatown, the Sunset District and so on and so forth and so white. To me, a thirteen-year-old Black girl, stalled by the South and Southern Black life style, the

city was a state of beauty and a state of freedom. The fog wasn't simply the steamy vapors off the Bay caught and penned in by hills, but a soft breath of anonymity that shrouded and cushioned the bashful traveler. I became dauntless and free of fears, intoxicated by the physical fact of San Francisco. Safe in my protecting arrogance, I was certain that no one loved her as impartially as I. I walked around the Mark Hopkins and gazed at the Top o' the Mark, but (maybe sour grapes) was more impressed by the view of Oakland from the hill than by the tiered building or its fur-draped visitors. For weeks, after the city and I came to terms about my belonging, I haunted the points of interest and found them empty and un-San Francisco. The naval officers with their well-dressed wives and clean white babies inhabited another time-space dimension than I. The well-kept old women in chauffeured cars and blond girls in buckskin shoes and cashmere sweaters might have been San Franciscans, but they were at most gilt on the frame of my portrait of the city.

Pride and Prejudice stalked in tandem the beautiful hills. Native San Franciscans, possessive of the city, had to cope with an influx, not of awed respectful tourists but of raucous unsophisticated provincials. They were also forced to live with skin-deep guilt brought on by the treatment of their former Nisei schoolmates.

Southern white illiterates brought their biases intact to the West from the hills of Arkansas and the swamps of Georgia. The Black ex-farmers had not left their distrust and fear of whites which history had taught them in distressful lessons. These two groups were obliged to work side by side in the war plants, and their animosities festered and opened like boils on the face of the city.

San Franciscans would have sworn on the Golden Gate Bridge that racism was missing from the heart of their air-conditioned city. But they would have been sadly mistaken.

A story went the rounds about a San Franciscan white matron who refused to sit beside a Negro civilian on the streetcar, even after he made room for her on the seat. Her explanation was that she would not sit beside a draft dodger who was a Negro as well. She added that the least he could do was fight for his country the way her son was fighting on Iwo Jima. The story said that the man pulled his body away from the window to show an armless sleeve. He said quietly and with great dignity, "Then ask you son to look around for my arm which I left over there."

215

Sourdough Bread

While this bread actually dates back to ancient times, it has been wildly popular in California since the days of the Gold Rush. Sourdough bread, unlike commercially baked white breads, is made with a starter. Before yeast was readily available, these starters were used as leavens in bread because they contained a combination of lactic bacteria and wild yeast. Starters have their own individual taste depending on where they were made, and the San Franciscan sourdough made from these starters is thought to have originated with Italian and French immigrants who traveled here from Mexico. Starters are something you can keep and add to for years, as well as pass along to friends. Don't be daunted by this recipe. Though the process is long, it is not difficult, and the results are delicious!

STARTER MIX:

1. In a small saucepan, over medium heat, bring the milk to a slow simmer.

2. Remove pan from heat, add water, and cool until mixture is lukewarm.

3. In a large bowl (large enough for both the ingredients and their expansion), combine sugar, salt, and flour. Add the milk-and-water mixture, and beat until well blended.

4. Cover with cheesecloth or a light, breathable towel and let stand in a warm place for 3-5 days, or until the mixture is bubbly and overwhelmingly pungent. (In truth, it's gonna stink!)

5. After 3-5 days, dissolve the yeast in the $\frac{1}{2}$ cup warm water and beat into starter.

6. Cover with a damp cloth and let stand at room temperature for a week, stirring daily. If starter looks like it is separating or curdling, don't worry, that's what you want. Just stir.

7. At the end of the week, remove cloth and place starter in a large jar or crock with a lid. It is now ready to be used.

8. You can replenish your starter as you use it, or pass it along to friends. For each $\frac{1}{2}$ cup of starter used, add $\frac{1}{2}$ cup flour and $\frac{1}{2}$ cup lukewarm water and stir. Even if the starter is not used, the same $\frac{1}{2}$ cup flour and water combination should be added weekly. The starter should be stirred daily and stored at room temperature for up to 3 days, otherwise it should be refrigerated.

STARTER MIX:

1 cup milk

1 cup water

1 tablespoon sugar

1 teaspoon salt

2 cups all-purpose flour

1 package active dry yeast

$\frac{1}{2}$ cup warm water

SPONGE:

SPONGE:

1. The night before baking, combine all sponge ingredients and beat well with a wooden spoon.

2. Cover with plastic wrap or cheesecloth and allow to stand overnight. (It should double in bulk.)

SOURDOUGH BREAD:

1. In a large bowl, combine yeast and water. Add the Sponge, followed by 1 cup of flour.

2. On a heavily floured surface, turn out dough and knead until it is very stiff, adding remaining 1 cup to 1½ cup of flour as you go. When finished, the dough should not be sticky at all.

3. Place in a greased bowl, cover and allow to rise for 1-2 hours, or until doubled in bulk.

4. Punch the dough down, cover again, and let rise 45 minutes to 1 hour longer.

5. On a lightly floured surface, turn out dough and divide in half.

6. If you are using bread pans, make sure they are well greased. If using a baking sheet, grease and sprinkle with cornmeal.

7. Place dough onto either baking sheet or bread pan. Slash several times across the top with a sharp knife. Allow to rise in a warm place 1 hour.

8. Arrange 2 racks in the middle of the oven. Preheat to 400°F. On the lower rack, place a shallow baking pan and fill with boiling water. Place bread on the higher rack.

9. Bake for 35-40 minutes, or until bread sounds hollow when tapped. Cool and serve.

MAKES 2 LOAVES

SPONGE:

1 cup warm water
1 cup starter
2 teaspoons sugar
2 teaspoons salt
4 cups flour

SOURDOUGH BREAD:

1 package dry yeast
½ cup warm water
Sourdough Sponge
(see above)
2-2½ cups flour

AT THE HEIGHT of the Great Depression, visionaries at the west edge of America were dreaming of ways to span San Francisco Bay. A seemingly impossible feat, this colossal undertaking would ultimately spawn two simultaneous projects: the first to connect San Francisco with Oakland, and the second to link the city with its northern neighbors.

SPANNING THE BAY: BUILDING THE BRIDGES OF SAN FRANCISCO

A bridge connecting San Francisco and Oakland had been imagined ever since the Gold Rush, but was always deemed financially and architecturally impossible. The deep waters and murky bay bottom presented numerous engineering issues, and the distance between the two cities (four and a half miles) seemed too far to connect. The advent of mass-produced automobiles and the volume of commuters (over 46 million people rode the ferries in 1928) led to the creation of the Toll Bridge Authority, charged with making the Bay Bridge a reality. The Authority appointed engineer Charles Purcell to map out the design and construction of the bridge.

On the other side of San Francisco, an engineer named Joseph Strauss worked to convince the city to build a bridge across the Golden Gate. For

nearly twelve years, he battled opposition from ferryboat operators and the military before he won their support for the bridge. Since all available municipal funds had already been allocated to the Bay Bridge project, six counties formed the Golden Gate Bridge and Highway District to raise money. Residents ratified a $35 million bond to fund the construction, which began on January 5, 1933.

Meanwhile, construction was well underway on the San Francisco—Oakland Bay Bridge. Between the two shores stood Yerba Buena Island, which would serve as an anchorage for the bridges spanning to the two cities. To cross the distance and deep waters between San Francisco and the island would still require creative engineering on scale yet to be seen. An enormous concrete pier was built at the midpoint to anchor two separate suspension bridges, which would connect San Francisco with Yerba Buena Island. When completed, the pier contained more concrete than the Empire State Building. Four suspension towers were built, two on each side of the anchorage, and two cables nearly 29 inches in diameter were fabricated to support the 37 million pounds of load from the two bridges.

To connect Yerba Buena and Oakland, the deepest bridge pier ever built was constructed to support the longest cantilevered span built to date. A tunnel through Yerba Buena Island connected the two bridges. At 56 feet high and 76 feet wide, it is still listed in the *Guinness Book of World Records* as the largest diameter bore tunnel in the world.

The Golden Gate Bridge had significant engineering challenges of its own to face. It needed to withstand high winds, turbulent seas, dense fog, and possible earthquakes as it was being constructed less than eight miles from the site of the devastating earthquake of 1906. Strauss built one bridge tower on bedrock at the north end, and the other anchored to an enormous ocean pier at the south end. Once the towers were completed, the cables were spun into place with enough wires to circle the globe three times. The Golden Gate is strong enough to support the weight of trucks and cars jammed bumper to bumper in every lane, and pedestrians in every inch of walkway, even in gale-force winds. It's also flexible enough to withstand a sway of 21 feet and sag of 10 feet.

Though these two projects had the most stringent safety precautions to date, many workers lost their lives during the course of construction. At a time when it was common for one person to die for every million dollars spent, 24 men died building the $77 million Bay Bridge, while 11 men lost their lives construction the $33 million Golden Gate. Nineteen men were saved by a safety net under the floor of the Golden Gate Bridge. They nicknamed themselves the Halfway to Hell Club.

The San Francisco—Oakland Bay Bridge opened on November 12, 1936, and was so popular that the number of automobiles immediately exceeded expectations. The bridge was first designed to carry passenger cars on its upper deck and rail traffic on the lower deck, but the railroads were eventually removed to make more room for cars. On May 27, 1937, the Golden Gate Bridge opened to much fanfare. Upon its completion, Joseph Strauss, who spent years dreaming of this day, penned a poem entitled "The Mighty Task Is Done" (see page 238). The Golden Gate's graceful design has become a San Francisco landmark and one of the world's most renowned bridges.

Together with the San Francisco—Oakland Bay Bridge, these two iconic structures carry nearly 400,000 vehicles a day. They are monuments to the ingenuity of those who dared to challenge convention, and remain an indispensable part of San Francisco's skyline.

I left my heart
In San Francisco.
High on a hill, it calls to me.
To be where little cable cars
climb halfway to the stars!
The morning fog may chill the air;
I don't care!

My love waits there
in San Francisco,
above the blue and windy sea.
When I come home to you, San Francisco,
your golden sun will shine for me!

I LEFT MY HEART IN
SAN FRANCISCO

Lyrics by DOUGLAS CROSS

WHAT'S SHAKIN'? CALIFORNIA QUAKES

The deadliest earthquake in U. S. history was the Great Earthquake of 1906 in San Francisco. The quake and resulting fires destroyed huge portions of the city and killed 3,000 people.

Southern California experiences about 10,000 earthquakes each year, most so small no one even feels them. A few hundred register higher than 3.0 on the Richter scale, and only 15–20 earthquakes register higher than 4.0.

Though world famous for its geologic activity, California does NOT have the most earthquakes every year in the U.S.—that honor goes to Alaska. California does, however, have the most damaging earthquakes every year due to a higher population and amount of infrastructure.

Los Angeles and San Francisco are creeping steadily toward each other along the San Andreas Fault at the lightning pace of two inches per year!

(That's just about the same speed as your fingernails grow.) At this rate, the two cities will be adjacent to each other in about 15 million years.

❈ ❈ ❈

The San Andreas Fault is not one continuous fault line, but a fault zone made up of numerous fault segments that stretch more than 800 miles through California. Movement and earthquakes can happen anywhere in that zone, and the faults can reach up to 10 miles deep in places.

❈ ❈ ❈

In 1895, geologist A.C. Lawson named the San Andreas Fault after San Andreas Lake, a pond about 20 miles south of San Francisco through which it runs. At the time, he didn't realize it stretched nearly the whole length of California!

❈ ❈ ❈

Contrary to rumors, California will NOT eventually fall into the ocean. The San Andreas Fault, which runs from the Salton Sea in the south to Cape Mendocino in the north, is the border between the Pacific plate (moving north) and North American plate (moving south). As they slip past each other, earthquakes result, but pressure keeps them pressed against each other. Consequently, Angelenos and San Franciscans could one day wind up as neighbors, but California will still be intact.

❈ ❈ ❈

Tsunamis are caused when an earthquake or landslide violently displaces ocean water. These waves can go unnoticed in deep water but move at speeds of up to 550 miles per hour and can move from one side of an ocean to the other in less than a day. As they approach a coast, the waves slow but grow up to 100 feet. When they come crashing down on shore, they can carry loose objects or people back out to sea.

❈ ❈ ❈

One of the largest tsunamis ever recorded was caused by an underwater quake and produced a wave over 1700 feet high in Lituya Bay, Alaska in 1958.

FROM FROM SEA TO SEA

BY RUDYARD KIPLING

"You want to go to the Palace Hotel?" said an affable youth on a dray. "What in hell are you doing here, then? This is about the lowest place in the city. Go six blocks north to corner of Geary and Market; then walk around till you strike corner of Gutter and Sixteenth, and that brings you there."

I do not vouch for the literal accuracy of these directions, quoting but from a disordered memory.

"Amen," I said, "But who am I that I should strike the corners of such as you name? Peradventure they be gentlemen of repute, and might hit back. Bring it down to dots, my son."

I thought he would have smitten me, but he didn't. He explained that no one ever used the word "street," and that everyone was supposed to know how the streets run; for sometimes the names were upon the lamps and sometimes they weren't. Fortified with these directions I proceeded till I found a light street full of sumptuous buildings four or five stories high, but paved with rude cobblestones in the fashion of the Year One. A cable car without any visible means of support slid stealthily behind me and nearly struck me in the back. A hundred yards further there was a slight commotion in the street—a gathering together of three or four— and something that glittered as it moved very swiftly. A ponderous Irish

gentleman with priest's cords in his hat and a small nickel-plated badge
on his fat bosom emerged from the knot, supporting a Chinaman who
had been stabbed in the eye and was bleeding like a pig. The bystanders
went their ways, and the Chinaman, assisted by the policeman, his own.
Of course this was none of my business, but I rather wanted to know
what had happened to the gentleman who had dealt the stab. It said a
great deal for the excellence of the municipal arrangements of the town
that a surging crowd did not at once block the street to see what was going
forward. I was the sixth man and the last who assisted at the performance,
and my curiosity was six times the greatest. Indeed, I felt ashamed of
showing it.

There were no more incidents till I reached the Palace Hotel, a seven-
storied warren of humanity with a thousand rooms in it. All the travel
books will tell you about hotel arrangements in this country. They should
be seen to be appreciated. Understand clearly—and this letter is written
after a thousand miles of experiences—that money will not buy you service
in the West.

When the hotel clerk—the man who awards your room to you and who
is supposed to give you information—when that resplendent individual
stoops to attend to your wants, he does so whistling or humming, or
picking his teeth, or pauses to converse with some one he knows. These
performances, I gather, are to impress upon you that he is a free man and
your equal. From his general appearance and the size of his diamonds
he ought to be your superior. There is no necessity for this swaggering

self-consciousness of freedom. Business is business, and the man who is paid to attend to a man might reasonable devote his whole attention to the job.

In a vast marble-paved hall under the glare of an electric light sat forty or fifty men; and for their use and amusement were provided spittoons of infinite capacity and generous gape. Most of the men wore frock coats and top hats—the things that we in India put on at a wedding breakfast if we possessed them—but they all spat. The spat on principle. The spittoons were on the staircases, in each bedroom—yea, and in chambers even more sacred than these. They chased one into retirement, but they blossomed in chiefest splendor round the Bar, and they were all used, every reeking one of 'em. Just before I began to feel deathly sick, another reporter grappled me. What he wanted to know was the precise area of India in square miles. I referred him to Whittaker. He had never heard of Whittaker. He wanted it from my own mouth, and I would not tell him. Then he swerved off, like the other man, to details of journalism in our own country. I ventured to suggest that the interior economy of a paper most concerned the people who worked it. "That's the very thing that interest us," he said. "Have you got reporters anything like our reporters on Indian newspapers?" "We have not," I said, and suppressed the "thank God" rising to my lips. "*Why* haven't you?" said he. "Because they would die," I said. It was exactly like talking to a child—a very rude little child. He would begin almost every sentence with: "Now tell me something about India," and would turn aimlessly from one question to

another without the least continuity. I was not angry, but keenly interested. The man was a revelation to me. To his questions I returned answers mendacious and evasive. After all, it really did not matter what I said. He could not understand. I can only hope and pray that none of the readers of the *Pioneer* will ever see that portentous interview. The man made me out to be an idiot several sizes more drivelling than my destiny intended, and the rankness of his ignorance managed to distort the few poor facts with which I supplied him into large and elaborate lies. Then thought I: "The matter of American journalism shall be looked into later on. At present I will enjoy myself."

No man rose to tell me what were the lions of the place. No one volunteered any sort of conveyance. I was absolutely alone in this big city of white folk. By instinct I sought refreshment and came upon a barroom full of bad Salon pictures, in which men with hats on the backs of their heads were wolfing food from a counter. It was the institution of the "Free Lunch" that I had struck. You paid for a drink and got as much as you wanted to eat. For something less than a rupee a day a man can feed himself sumptuously in San Francisco, even though he be bankrupt. Remember this if ever you are stranded in these parts.

Later, I began a vast but unsystematic exploration of the streets. I asked for no names. It was enough that the pavements were full of white men and women, the streets clanging with traffic, and that the restful roar of a great city rang in my ears. The cable cars glided to all points of the compass. I took them one by one till I could go no farther. San

Francisco has been pitched down on the sand bunkers of the Bikaneer desert. About one-fourth of it is ground reclaimed from the sea—any old-timer will tell you all about that. The remainder is ragged, unthrifty sand hills, pegged down by houses.

From an English point of view there has not been the least attempt at grading those hills, and indeed you might as well try to grade the hillocks of Sind. The cable cars have for all practical purposes made San Francisco a dead level. They take no count of rise or fall, but slide equably on their appointed course from one end to the other of a six-mile street. They turn corners almost at right angles; cross other lines, and, for aught I know, may run up the sides of houses. There is no visible agency of their flight; but once in a while you shall pass a five-storied building, humming with machinery that winds up an everlasting wire cable, and the initiated will tell you that here is the mechanism. I gave up asking questions. If it pleases Providence to make a car run up and down a slit in the ground for many miles, and if for twopence-halfpenny I can ride in that car, why shall I seek the reasons of the miracle? Rather let me look out of the windows till the shops give place to thousands and thousands of little houses made of wood—each house just big enough for a man and his family. Let me watch the people in the cars, and try to find out in what manner they differ from us, their ancestors. They delude themselves into the belief that they talk English—*the* English—and I have already been pitied for speaking with "an English accent." The man who pitied me spoke, so far as I was concerned, the language of thieves. And they all do.

Night fell over the Pacific, and the white sea-fog whipped through the streets, dimming the splendors of the electric lights. It is the use of this city, her men and women, to parade between the hours of eight and ten a certain street, called Kearney Street, where the finest shops are situated. Here the click of heels on the pavement is loudest, here the lights are brightest, and here the thunder of the traffic is most overwhelming. I watched Young California and saw that it was at least expensively dressed, cheerful in manner, and self-asserting in conversation. Also the women are very fair. The maidens were of generous build, large, well groomed, and attired in raiment that even to my inexperienced eyes must have cost much. Kearney Street, at nine o'clock, levels all distinctions of rank as impartially as the grave. Again and again I loitered at the heels of a couple of resplendent beings, only to overhear, when I expected the level voice of culture, the staccato "Sez he," "Sez I," that is the mark of the white servant girl all the world over.

This was depressing because, in spite of all that goes to the contrary, fine feathers ought to make fine birds. There was wealth—unlimited wealth—in the streets, but not an accent that would not have been dear at fifty cents. Wherefore, revolving in my mind that these folk were barbarians, I was presently enlightened and made aware that they also were the heirs of all the ages, and civilized after all.

AWAY ABOVE A HARBORFUL

By Lawrence Ferlinghett

Away above a harborful
                of caulkless houses
among the charley noble chimneypots
                  of a rooftop rigged with clotheslines
a woman pastes up sails
              upon the wind
hanging out her morning sheets
                with wooden pins
        O lovely mammal
                her nearly naked teats
      throw taut shadows
              when she stretches up
to hang at last the last of her
            so white washed sins
but it is wetly amorous
            and winds itself about her
clinging to her skin

                              So caught with arms upraised
          she tosses back her head
                              in voiceless laughter
          and in choiceless gesture then
                              shakes out gold hair

while in the reachless seascape spaces

                              between the blown white shrouds

          stand out the bright steamers

                              to kingdom come

Crab Louis

¹⁄₂ cup good-quality mayonnaise

2 teaspoons Dijon mustard

¹⁄₂ teaspoon Worcestershire sauce

Juice of 1 lemon, save cut halves for later

¹⁄₄ cup chili sauce

¹⁄₄ cup finely chopped scallions

4 large green stuffed olives, chopped

Salt and pepper to taste

1 pound crab meat, cut into chunks

4 ripe avocados

Iceberg lettuce, shredded

4 hard boiled eggs

4 ripe tomatoes, quartered or chopped

THOUGH THE ORIGINS OF THIS DELICIOUS DISH ARE SHROUDED IN MYSTERY, THERE IS NO DOUBT THAT IT IS A CLASSIC CALIFORNIA FAVORITE. MOST FOOD HISTORIANS AGREE THAT THIS CRAB CONCOCTION BECAME POPULAR IN THE EARLY PART OF THE 20TH CENTURY, AND BOTH SOLARI'S RESTAURANT AND THE ST. FRANCIS HOTEL OF SAN FRANCISCO CLAIM TO BE THE CREATORS OF THE "KING OF SALADS." WHILE VARIATIONS ON THIS RECIPE ABOUND, OUR VERSION SERVES UP THE DIVINELY DRESSED CRAB ON ANOTHER CALIFORNIA CLASSIC, THE AVOCADO.

1. In a mixing bowl combine mayonnaise, mustard, Worcestershire sauce, and lemon juice.

2. When thick and smooth, add the chili sauce, scallions and olives. Mix well and season to taste with salt and pepper.

3. In a large mixing bowl, add crab and half the sauce. Mix gently so as not to break up the crab lumps.

4. Split the avocados in half and discard the pits. Using the reserved lemon halves, rub exposed avocado flesh to prevent discoloration.

5. Pile equal portions of the crab into the avocado halves. Spoon remaining dressing over the crab. Place on a bed of iceberg lettuce.

6. Garnish with egg slices and tomatoes and serve immediately.

SERVES 2

ALCATRAZ: THE ROCK

IN 1775, Spanish explorer Lieutenant Juan Manuel de Ayala charted the San Francisco Bay and named a rocky island (said to be white from bird dung) "Isla de los Alcatraces" or "Island of the Pelicans." Around the time of the Gold Rush, in the 1850s, the United States military arrived to build Fort Alcatraz. Though originally constructed for defense, the fort rapidly became a popular repository for local military men accused of deserting, robbing, or drinking to excess. In 1861, Alcatraz was named the official military prison for the Department of the Pacific.

When the Civil War erupted in 1861, Confederate sympathizers and civilians accused of treason joined military prisoners on Alcatraz. Native Americans who clashed with U. S. authorities, Philippine prisoners of the Spanish-American War, and World War I conscientious objectors were also imprisoned there. As its old guns became obsolete, the fort's defensive value was clearly waning. In 1912, a mammoth new prison, also known as "The Rock," was completed, but when the Great Depression hit in the early 1930s, high costs forced the military to hand over operations to the Federal Bureau of Prisons. To calm public fears of rising crime rates and increasingly bold gangsters, the government created United States Penitentiary (USP) Alcatraz, a maximum-security super-prison where the nation's most incorrigible inmates could be contained and strictly controlled. The swift currents and cold water (53°F) surrounding Alcatraz, as well as the island's distance from shore (1.5 miles), made Alcatraz virtually inescapable.

But men still tried to get away. Over 28 years, 36 prisoners attempted to break out; twenty-three were recaptured, six were shot and killed, two drowned, and five are missing and presumed drowned. The bloodiest escape attempt occurred in 1946 when six prisoners took control of the cellhouse, beginning what became known as the "Battle of Alcatraz." In the end, two guards and three inmates were killed, and 17 guards and one inmate were injured. Two of the three surviving convicts who took part in the escape were later executed.

Another bold escape attempt was immortalized in Clint Eastwood's *Escape from Alcatraz*. On the morning of June 12, 1962, guards found life-like dummies (complete with human hair) in the bunks of three inmates. An investigation revealed the men had escaped using homemade drills to enlarge vent holes in their cells, false wall-and-vent segments to hide their work, and a raft fashioned from prison-issue raincoats. In the water, searchers found two homemade life vests and some carefully waterproofed letters and photos. Several weeks later, a man dressed in a blue prisonlike uniform washed up near San Francisco, but the body was too badly decomposed to be identified. In spite of an exhaustive investigation by the FBI, the three men were never officially located and are presumed drowned.

Other infamous prisoners included Al "Scarface" Capone,* George "Machine Gun" Kelly, Doc Barker of the Ma Barker gang, "Public Enemy No. 1" Alvin Karpis, political prisoner Morton Sobell, and Robert Stroud, "the Birdman of Alcatraz." In its 29 years of operation, USP Alcatraz housed 1,545 prisoners. On March 21, 1963, high operating and repair costs forced the prison to close for good.

Today, Alcatraz Island is run by the National Park Service as part of the Golden Gate National Recreation Area. Almost a million visitors per year explore what remains of the prison and its gardens, discover the island's protected-bird sanctuary and tide pools, and revel in Alcatraz's beautiful bay vistas.

*Contrary to persistent rumors, San Francisco Bay contains no "man-eating" sharks, Al Capone did not die at Alcatraz, and "the Birdman of Alcatraz" never kept birds on the island. He raised and studied them while imprisoned in Leavenworth, before arriving at Alcatraz.

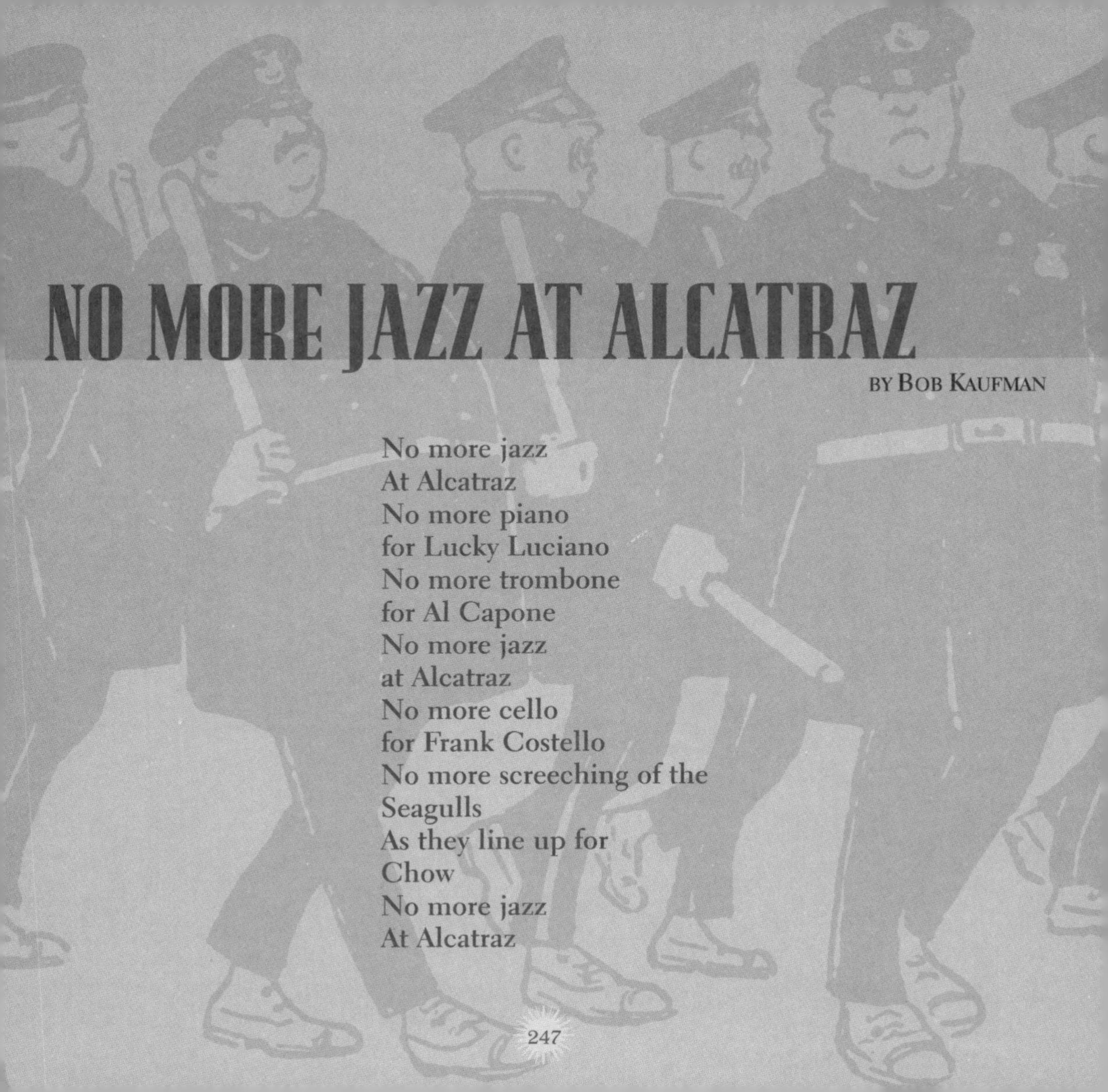

NO MORE JAZZ AT ALCATRAZ

BY BOB KAUFMAN

No more jazz
At Alcatraz
No more piano
for Lucky Luciano
No more trombone
for Al Capone
No more jazz
at Alcatraz
No more cello
for Frank Costello
No more screeching of the
Seagulls
As they line up for
Chow
No more jazz
At Alcatraz

WHEN I CAME TO SAN FRANCISCO, the city was just exploding with this counterculture movement. I thought, "This is it!" It was like paradise there. Everybody was in love with life and in love with their fellow human beings to the point where they were just sharing in incredible ways with everybody. Taking people in off the street and letting them stay in their homes, breaking free of conventional morality. You could walk down almost any street in Haight-Ashbury where I was living, and someone would smile at you and just go, "Hey, it's beautiful, isn't it?" It was like people were high on the street and willing to share that energy. It was a very special time.

"...THERE IS THIS ILLUSION OF ABUNDANCE HERE...."

FROM **HIPPIES**

BY ALEX FORMAN

It was a whole other vision of what was possible. Rents were cheap and people were living in big communal groups, and we didn't have to work very hard. There was a sense that you didn't need very much, and that people who worked hard were just trapped into trying to acquire more and more possessions. People should just begin more to enjoy life, play music, dance, experience nature. We were going to raise our kids communally and all that stuff, and such attitudes would flourish even more. I thought this was the new world beginning right here—an alternative society—and this was where I wanted to be. So I stayed.

The first human Be-In was in January of '67 in Golden Gate Park. That was a very high moment. People went and just kind of experienced. A lot of people were on LSD or peyote or marijuana. They played music, shared food, played drums, did American Indian chanting. You know, tie-dyed clothes, the whole thing. It all seems very trite now, but at the time it was all new. People were coming from all over the world to research it, to experience it. People from Czechoslovakia, Australia, Finland. It was a real phenomenon.

For a while I worked with a group in the Haight called the Diggers, who had a kind of a primitive communism view that was just "share all the wealth." The Diggers set up a free store, and people could just come in and take whatever they needed, and we fed people for free in the park. At one point I realized the absurdity of that when these people from the neighborhood, these older black women, came into the free store and said, "How much do these clothes cost in here?"

We said, "Oh, it's all free. You just take what you need, and then if you have extra, you give."

They said, "What do you mean, you just take what you need?"

"Well, you just take what you need, that's all."

They said, "Really?"

So they came back with these big boxes and they started just taking tons of stuff off the racks.

We said, "What are you doing?"

They said, "Well, you said take what you need."

We said, "Yeah, well, you don't need all those clothes for yourself."

They said, "No, but we need the money, so we're going to take the clothes and sell them."

They were in real scarcity, you know, they needed money, and here we were saying just take what you need for your own personal, immediate needs. But for them, that wasn't reality. Their reality was, "How are we going to get some money, and here's these foolish white people just letting us take whatever we need. Well, we need it all. We don't have anything."

That was the illusion of the whole hippie ethos, that there was this abundance. I think the hippie movement started in California—and was most powerful here—because there is this illusion of abundance here. Fruits were falling from the trees, rent was cheap, there were places to stay, the weather was tolerable even in the winter, there was a community of people who were into sharing. But there wasn't an abundance. There was an abundance at a certain time for certain people.

In early 1967, people would just give things away. On every street corner, there would be somebody giving things away, free food, a free place to stay. Then in the summer of '67 was the Summer of Love. People started storming in by the thousands, and within three months there were people begging, "Do you have free food?" In other words, so many came that the surplus changed to scarcity. It got very ugly very fast. People got into really bad drugs like speed and heroin. There were ripoffs, violence, guns being drawn, people really malnourished, hepatitis, people living on the street with no place to stay.

I quickly saw then that the counterculture wasn't going to make it. It wasn't going to work. It was an illusion. And meanwhile the war was going on. It became more and more clear that you couldn't just set up little islands of peace and love in the middle of the Vietnam War.

TAKING THE PLUNGE

BY *AMISTEAD MAUPIN*

Mary Ann Singleton was twenty-five years old when she saw San Francisco for the first time.

She came the city alone for an eight-day vacation. On the fifth night, she drank three Irish coffees at the Buena Vista, realized that her mood ring was blue, and decided to phone her mother in Cleveland.

"Hi, Mom. It's me."

Oh, darling. Your daddy and I were just talking about you. There was this crazy man on McMillan and Wife who was strangling all these secretaries, and I just couldn't help thinking…"

"Mom…"

"I know. Just crazy ol' Mom, worrying herself sick over nothing. But you never can tell about those things. Look at that poor Patty Hearst, locked up in that closet with all those awful…"

"Mom…long distance."

"Oh…yes. You must be having a grand time."

"God…you wouldn't believe it! The people here are so friendly I feel like I've…"

"Have you been to the Top of the Mark like I told you?"

"Not yet."

"Well, don't you dare miss that! You know, your daddy took me there when he got back from the South Pacific. I remember he slipped the

bandleader five dollars, so we could dance to 'Moonlight Serenade,' and I spilled Tom Collins all over his beautiful white Navy…"

"Mom, I want you to do me a favor."

"Of course, darling. Just listen to me. Oh…before I forget it, I ran into Mr. Lassiter yesterday at the Ridgemont Mall, and he said the office is just falling apart with you gone. They don't get many good secretaries at Lassiter Fertilizers."

"Mom, that's sort of why I called."

"Yes, darling?"

"I want you to call Mr. Lassiter and tell him I won't be in on Monday morning."

"Oh…Mary Ann, I'm not sure you should ask for an extension on your vacation."

"It's not an extension, Mom."

"Well, then why…?"

"I'm not coming home, Mom."

Silence. Then, dimly in the distance, a television voice began to tell Mary Ann's father about the temporary relief of hemorrhoids. Finally, her mother spoke: "Don't be silly, darling."

"Mom…I'm not being silly. I *like* it here. It feels like home already."

"Mary Ann, if there's a boy…"

"There's no boy.…I've thought about this for a long time."

"Don't be ridiculous! You've been there five days!"

"Mom, I know how you feel, but…well, it's got nothing to do with you and Daddy. I just want to start making my own life…have my own apartment and all."

"Oh, *that.* Well, darling…of *course* you can. As a matter of fact, your daddy and I thought those new apartments out at Ridgemont might be just perfect for you. They take lots of young people, and they've got a swimming pool and a sauna, and I could make some of those darling curtains like I made for Sonny and Vicki when they got married. You could have all the privacy you…"

"You aren't listening, Mom. I'm trying to tell you I'm a grown woman."

"Well, act like it, then! You can't just…run away from your family and friends to go live with a bunch of hippies and mass murderers!"

"You've been watching too much TV."

"O.K.…then what about The Horoscope?"

"Mom…The Zodiac."

"Same difference. And what about…earthquakes? I saw that movie, Mary Ann, and I nearly died when Ava Gardner…"

"Will you just call Mr. Lassiter for me"

Her mother began to cry. "You won't come back. I just know it."

"Mom…please…I will. I promise."

"But you won't be…the same!"

"No. I hope not."

California, Here I Come,
Right back where I started from.
Where bowers of flowers bloom in the sun.
Each morning at dawning birdies sing and ev'rything.
A sunkissed miss said, "Don't be late."
That's why I can hardly wait.
Open up that golden gate;
California, Here I Come!

CALIFORNIA, HERE I COME

BY AL JOLSON, B.G. DeSYLVA, AND JOSEPH MEYER

TAHOE IN AUGUST

BY ROBERT HASS

What summer proposes is simply happiness:
heat early in the morning, jays
raucous in the pines. Frank and Ellen have a tennis game
at nine, Bill and Cheryl sleep on the deck
to watch a shower of summer stars. Nick and Sharon
stayed in, sat and talked the dark on,
drinking tea, and Jeanne walked into the meadow
in a white smock to write in her journal
by a grazing horse who seemed to want the company.
Some of them will swim in the afternoon.
Someone will drive to the hardware store to fetch
new latches for the kitchen door. Four o'clock;
the joggers jogging—it is one of them who sees
down the flowering slope the woman with her notebook
in her hand beside the white horse, gesturing, her hair
from a distance the copper color of the hummingbirds
the slant light catches on the slope; the hikers
switchback down the canyon from the waterfall;

the readers are reading, Anna is about to meet Vronsky,
that nice M. Swann is dining in Combray
with the aunts, and Carrie has come to Chicago.
What they want is happiness: someone to love them,
children, a summer by the lake. The woman who sets aside
her book blinks against the fuzzy dark,
re-entering the house. Her daughter drifts downstairs;
out late the night before, she has been napping,
and she's cross. Her mother tells her David telephoned.
"He's such a dear," the mother says, "I think
I make him nervous." The girl tosses her head as the horse
had done n the meadow while Jeanne read it her dream.
"You can call him now, if you want," the mother says,
"I've got to get the chicken started,

I won't listen." "Did I say you would?"
the girls says quickly. The mother who has been slapped
this way before and done the same herself another summer
on a different lake says, "Ouch." The girl shrugs
sulkily. "I'm sorry." Looking down: "Something
about the way you said that pissed me off."
"Hannibal has wandered off," the mother says,
wryness in her voice, she is thinking it is August,
"why don't you see if he's at the Finleys' house
again." The girl says, "God." The mother: "He loves
small children. It's livelier for him there."
The daughter, awake now, flounces out the door,
which slams. It is for all of them the sound of summer.
The mother she looks like stands at the counter snapping beans.

The redwoods seem not to have really accepted the loss of the dinosaurs. In their silence they seem to wait for footsteps unheard these sixty million years.

—David Rains Wallace

FAMOUS CALIFORNIANS

YOU'LL FIND LOTS OF FAMILIAR NAMES HERE—from actors and actresses to athletes and authors, people who have risen to the top of their professions and infused their lives with a bit of that pioneering spirit that has characterized Californians for centuries—but you will notice some of your favorites are missing. Why? Because while thousands have made their fortunes in the Golden State, our list requires that each entrant be California born and bred, through and through.

❈ ❈ ❈

Ansel Adams—photographer
(San Francisco)

Marcus Allen—football player
(San Diego)

Shirley Temple Black—actress,
ambassador *(Santa Monica)*

Brian Boitano—Olympic Skater
(Mountain View)

Julia Child—chef, television
personality *(Pasadena)*

Jackie Coogan—actor *(Los Angeles)*

Coolio—rap artist *(Los Angeles)*

Oscar De La Hoya—boxer
(East Los Angeles)

Leonardo DiCaprio—actor *(Hollywood)*

Joe DiMaggio—baseball player *(Martinez)*

Clint Eastwood—actor, director
(San Francisco)

Isadora Duncan—dancer *(San Francisco)*

Robert Frost—poet *(San Francisco)*

Jeff Gordon—race car driver *(Vallejo)*

Florence Griffith-Joyner—Olympic Track
and Field *(Los Angeles)*

William Randolph Hearst—publisher
(San Francisco)

Mariel Hemingway—actress
(Mill Valley)

Anthony M. Kennedy—jurist *(Sacramento)*

Jack London—author *(San Francisco)*

Greg Louganis—Olympic diver
(San Diego)

George Lucas—filmmaker *(Modesto)*

Mark McGwire—baseball player *(Pomona)*

Richard M. Nixon—U. S. president
(Yorba Linda)

George S. Patton, Jr.—general
(San Gabriel)

Robert Redford—actor *(Santa Monica)*

Sally K. Ride—astronaut *(Encino)*

William Saroyan—author *(Fresno)*

John Steinbeck—author *(Salinas)*

Adlai Stevenson—statesman
(Los Angeles)

Amy Tan—author *(Oakland)*

Michael Tilson Thomas—conductor
(Hollywood)

Earl Warren—jurist *(Los Angeles)*

Serena and Venus Williams—
tennis players *(Lynwood)*

Eldrick "Tiger" Woods—
golfer *(Cypress)*

Kristi Yamaguchi—Olympic gold medal
winner ice skater *(Hayward)*

California Rolls

3 ¹⁄₃ cups rice

5 ¹⁄₃ tablespoons rice wine vinegar

5 tablespoons sugar

3 tablespoons salt

1 makisu (sushi rolling mat)

10 sheets seaweed, halved

¹⁄₂ pound fresh or imitation crab (if using imitation "Krab," cut into long, thin pieces)

1 cucumber, peeled, seeded, and julienned.

1 avocado, peeled, seeded, and cut into long, thin pieces

Sesame seeds, optional

With Japanese culture so much a part of California, it's no surprise that sushi has become such a popular food. Legend has it that in the 1970s, a smart California chef realized that Americans were having a tough time warming up to the concept of eating raw fish, so he created a sushi treat more in tune with their palettes. Here is a sushi recipe to try if you have always wanted to make the dish, but were unsure about getting the freshest fish or the right supplies. Specialty food markets carry the seaweed and the makisu mat used to roll the sushi.

1. Wash the rice until the water rinses clear. Drain in a colander and let it stand for 30 minutes.

2. Place rice in a pot or rice cooker, and add 4 cups of water or follow the instructions on a rice cooker. Bring the water to a boil. Reduce the heat to a simmer and cover the pot. Cook for 15 minutes. Remove the cover, place a damp towel over the rice, and let cool for 10 minutes.

3. Combine vinegar, salt, and sugar.

4. Pour vinegar over cooked rice and mix thoroughly.

5. Cover a makisu (sushi rolling mat) with plastic wrap. Place half of a sheet of the seaweed over the plastic on the mat.

6. Place a handful of rice across the seaweed and spread it evenly over the seaweed.

7. Place some of crab meat (or "Krab" meat) along the center of the rice.

8. Add cucumber and avocado along the center of the rice.

9. Using the mat and plastic wrap, roll the rice around the filling and press lightly to seal.

10. Remove the mat and plastic wrap and sprinkle the roll with sesame seeds. Cut the sushi roll into bite-size pieces. Repeat with the remaining ingredients. Serve.

Serves 6

MY MOTHER, Juana Estela Salgado de Scherr, came home from her English class and said, in Spanish, "I had a very interesting conversation with a Japanese woman while I was waiting for the bus." Her eyes glistened with amusement and she cupped her mouth when she laughed. "The woman came up to me and started speaking Japanese. I told her in Spanish that I did not speak Japanese. She laughed too. She thought I was Japanese." I could understand why—my mother's black black eyes, their Indian slant, straight black hair, cinnamon-and-lemon colored skin, cheekbones tilted toward the sun. My father's Baltimore Jewish family, who had never seen a Mexican before, said my mother "looks like Madame Chaing-Kai-Shek."

LA JAPONESA

BY RAQUEL SCHERR

In the 1950s, in Berkeley, foreign faces looked familial to me, rather like seeing an American in a Mexican town—an instantly familiar stranger. We lived in Albany's Codornices Village, on Sixth Street, a mostly Black neighborhood. My father, Max Scherr, often took me to the Piccolo, a popular coffee shop near the Berkeley campus where he'd meet his friends. They were mainly Jewish or Black. How different they seemed from college men with crewcuts

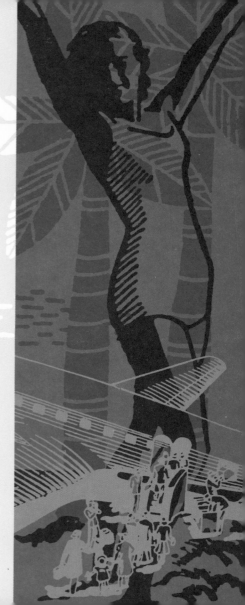

273

slicked in vasoline, and college women in tight skirts, cashmere sweaters, and duck-tailed hair. I thought they all came from places like Modesto. My friend Judy Nikaido referred to them as "white people." She was born in a detention camp in California. After the war a young white couple helped ease the Nikaidos' financial pressures by taking the youngest of seven children until things got better. When things got better, they refused to give her back. Nothing could be done because she didn't want to come back. Mrs. Nikaido cried in the corner of her living room which smelled strongly of incense, while Judy and I played Monopoly. Neither of our mothers spoke English.

I asked my mother how she was able to have a conversation with the woman at the bus stop. "A little Spanish, a little Japanese, a little English, and a lot of hands. We understood each other very well." She would always say this about the people in her classes. "We understand each other very well." She told me about her good friend, "el Peruano" (the Peruvian), who was putting himself through college and supporting his aunt and invalid mother by working at Larry Blake's restaurant, or about "la joven Pakistani" (the young Pakastani woman) who wanted to go back home, but her husband wanted to stay. There were also the Delgados, a Cuban family who came to California before the revolution. Their kids went to school with my brothers and me. They were the only "latinos," besides the Randalls' kids who were mixed like us, and my Mexican friend Gloria who insisted she was Spanish. In later years, my mother told me about "la Vietnames" whose husband was killed while carrying medical equipment in Saigon. She brought her son to the U.S., but left her small daughter behind. "And your father writing about hippies," my mother said, meaning the *Berkeley Barb*, an underground newspaper my father started in 1965.

My mother kept going back to school to practice her English; not to learn it but to be with friends: "el Colombiano," "la Nicaraguense," "la Koreana," "el Panameño," "la Japonesa," "la China," "la Filipina."

She had been in her last year of medical school at the University of Mexico when she met my father, a young lawyer who rode the rails to California, then hitchhiked to Mexico. My mother had read the Classics. Octavio Paz had been her schoolmate. Her first few years in Berkeley she wore long handpainted Mexican skirts and thickly colored embroidered blouses. "The whole world comes to my English class," she'd say. "The whole world comes to California. We understand each other very well." I think of her talking to the woman at the bus stop, and it seems, thousands of years ago, my Mexican mother—part Aztec, French, and Spanish—was Japanese.

THE CALIFORNIA REGION'S FIRST significant settlers were Spaniards. In the late 1700s, the Spaniards established a series of missions intended to Christianize the local tribes and secure Spanish influence. Though the Spanish priests maintained regional power for many decades, Spain largely neglected the colony. By 1820, only 3,750 Spanish citizens populated the area. Mexico won its independence from Spain in 1821, and by 1825, the Spanish Californians (Californios) had pledged their loyalty to Mexico.

CALIFORNIA'S IMMIGRANTS: SPANISH, CHINESE, JAPANESE, AND MEXICAN

The 1849 Gold Rush and an influx of Anglo-American settlers pushed California into statehood. Subsequently, the 10,000 Californios were identified as "foreigners" and forced off their lands. But the Californios' legacy lives on, reflected in Californian art, architecture,

music, and food. Many of California's most famous cities, such as Los Angeles, San Diego, San Francisco, and Monterey, still boast the names they were given by the first Spanish-speaking settlers. And the wine and citrus crops first harvested by the Californios still feed some of California's largest industries.

In addition to the dominant new population of Anglo Americans, other immigrant groups also left their mark on California. The first Chinese, drawn by the Gold Rush's Gam Sann, "Gold Mountain," arrived in 1848. As gold got harder to find, the state taxed foreign miners, and the Chinese were pushed into menial, low-wage jobs. They performed many essential tasks, building fishing ships, developing abalone and shrimp industries, laying the transcontinental tracks for the Central Pacific Railroad, and reclaiming swampland in the Sacramento Delta.

By 1867, roughly 50,000 Chinese lived in California. When an economic slump led to high unemployment in the 1870s, many Americans blamed their troubles on Asian immigrants who worked for low pay. Anti-Chinese riots pressured lawmakers to pass restrictive immigration laws. In 1882, the Chinese Exclusion Act temporarily barred all Chinese from immigrating, with the exception of those whose fathers or husbands were U.S. citizens. In 1888, the Scott Act went even further, barring all Chinese permanently, even those who had gone back to China to visit.

In 1910, California opened an immigration station on Angel Island in the San Francisco Bay. Though originally dubbed "the Ellis Island of the West," it was used mainly to control Chinese immigration. Over the next 30 years, some 175,000 Chinese were detained on the Island, and by 1920, the Chinese—American population was reduced by almost 50 percent. Congress soon passed the Immigration Restriction Act of 1924, excluding virtually all Asian immigrants. In 1943, the United States entered World War II as a Chinese ally and finally repealed the Chinese exclusion acts. But postwar fears of communism again stigmatized Chinese Americans, forcing many to assimilate completely into American culture and deny their traditional heritage.

The Immigration and Nationality Act of 1965 abolished the national-origins quota system, which had effectively limited Asian immigration to token levels. Chinese from Hong Kong, Taiwan, and, after 1979, mainland China began immigrating to California. Postwar immigrants were more likely to be political refugees, professionals, and intellectuals than recruited laborers. They often hailed from cities instead of the country, coming with their families instead of alone. Throughout California, this new influx of immigrants has reinforced long established Chinese-American communities, considerably advancing Chinese-American influence on politics, economics, and culture. San Francisco and Los Angeles have blossomed into major Chinese-American centers.

Another prominent group of immigrants were the Japanese. By 1885, following the Chinese Exclusion Act of 1882, large numbers of young, Japanese laborers began replacing Chinese as cheap laborers in the railroad, farming, and fishing industries. Growing anti-Japanese violence and legislation soon followed. A 1907 "Gentlemen's Agreement" between Japan and the United States restricted Japanese immigration and spawned more anti-Japanese sentiments. Between 1900 and 1910, the Japanese began establishing farms, vineyards, and orchards in central California. By 1920, they were firmly entrenched in farming, distributing, and retailing agricultural products. As the Japanese-American population steadily increased due to arranged marriages with "picture brides" from Japan and childbirth, anti-Japanese groups charged that the Japanese were inassimilable and capable of overrunning the state.

After Japan attacked Pearl Harbor and the United States entered the Second World War, both resident-alien Japanese and American citizens of Japanese descent were sent to guarded detention camps. From 1942 to 1945, over 120,000 Japanese Americans were incarcerated. After the war, Japanese-American communities, with economic losses conservatively estimated to be around $400 million, struggled to rebuild. In 1948, the Japanese-American Evacuation Claims Act paid out $38 million (about $2,500 per person) for their sufferings. During the 1950s, the Californian Japanese-American population almost doubled, due largely to third generation births. Many laborers transitioned from rural, agriculture-based work to urban jobs in technical, professional fields. In the late 1980s, the Civil Liberties Act of 1988 further compensated each internment survivor with an additional $20,000 in reparations, and Congress formally apologized.

Though modern day Mexican immigrants have also greatly affected California, their influence grew slowly. When their predecessors, the Californios, lost their lands, they also lost their political power and

livelihoods. In the second half of the 1800s, many Californios became poorly paid migratory laborers working in California's budding commercial-agriculture industry. Others moved to cities for construction, railroad, and food-processing jobs. During this time, few Mexicans immigrated to the United States. By the end of the 19th century, Spanish-speaking Californians had become a relatively powerless minority, facing discrimination and segregation.

But in 1910, a revolution in Mexico and the promise of better jobs in the United States drove thousands of Mexicans north. World War I increased the American need for immigrant workers. Between 1910 and 1930, more than 680,000 Mexicans moved to the United States. The Great Depression again reversed trends. Whereas nearly 500,000 Mexicans had immigrated in the 1920s, the 1930s saw only 32,700 follow suit. High unemployment caused Anglo-Americans to view Mexicans as "surplus labor" and forced roughly one half-million Mexican Americans to move back to Mexico. The cosponsored American—Mexican Repatriation Program applied additional pressure on Mexican immigrants to "voluntarily" return home.

World War II renewed the need for Mexican labor. In 1942, the United States and Mexican governments developed the Bracero (day laborer) program, which allowed Mexicans to work legally on U.S farms and railroads. Mexican immigration to the United States rose steeply during the 1950s, peaking at 450,000 workers in 1959.

Over the next few decades, illegal immigration continued to increase. California's population growth in the 1970s and 1980s resulted largely from illegal Mexican immigration. Population and immigration issues contributed to California's growing economic pressures. Social tensions increased, and illegal immigration was a topic of constant political debate. In 1994, California voters approved Proposition 187, barring the state from providing most services, such as education, welfare, and non-emergency medical care, to illegal immigrants. Federal courts later found much of the proposition unconstitutional.

Mexican Americans are now making educational, political, and social progress, playing an increasingly important role in California. Most studies estimate that within the next 20 to 30 years Mexican Americans and other Latinos will make up more than 50 percent of California's population. Mexican Americans enrich Californian and U.S. culture with their distinctive art, music, literature, theater, and films. In addition, Spanish-language media has exploded, resulting in two national, Spanish-language television networks and hundreds of Hispanic radio stations, newspapers, magazines, and journals.

The picturesque, bountiful California region has long served as a crossroads of America's newest cultures, absorbing immigrants from around the globe. From the farmers of Imperial Valley to Silicon Valley's high-tech gurus, these immigrants all add to the vibrant cultural fabric that is California today.

FROM THE WOMAN WARRIOR

BY MAXINE HONG KINGSTON

Reading out loud was easier than speaking because we did not have to make up what we say, but I stopped often, and the teacher would think I'd gone quiet again. I could not understand "I." The Chinese "I" has seven strokes, intricacies. How could the American "I," assuredly wearing a hat like the Chinese, have only three strokes, the middle so straight? Was it out of politeness that this writer left off strokes the way a Chinese has to write her own name small and crooked? No, it was not politeness; "I" is a capital and "you" is lower-case. I stared at that middle line and waited so long for its black center to resolve into tight strokes and dots that I forgot to pronounce it. The other troublesome word was "here," no strong consonant to hang on to, and so flat, when "here" is two mountainous ideographs. The teacher, who had already told me every day how to read "I" and "here," put me in the low corner under the stairs again, where the noisy boys usually sat.

When my second grade class did a play, the whole class went to the auditorium except the Chinese girls. The teacher, lovely and Hawaiian, should have understood about us, but instead left us behind in the class-room. Our voices were too soft or nonexistent, and our parents never signed the permission slips anyway. They never signed anything un-

necessary. We opened the door a crack and peeked out, but closed it again quickly. One of us (not me) won every spelling bee, though.

I remember telling the Hawaiian teacher, "We Chinese can't sing 'land where our fathers died.'" She argued with me about politics, while I meant because of curses. But how can I have that memory when I couldn't talk? My mother says that we, like ghosts, have no memories.

After American school, we picked up our cigar boxes, in which we had arranged books, brushes, and an inkbox neatly, and went to Chinese school, from 5:00 to 7:30 P.M. There we chanted together, voices rising and falling, loud and soft, some boys shouting, everybody reading together, reciting together and not alone with one voice. When we had a memorization test, the teacher let each of us come to his desk and say the lesson to him privately, while the rest of the class practiced copying or tracing. Most of the teachers were men. The boys who were so well behaved in the American school played tricks on them and talked back to them. The girls were not mute. They screamed and yelled during recess, when there were no rules; they had fistfights. Nobody was afraid of children hurting themselves or of children hurting school property. The glass doors to the red and green balconies with the gold joy symbols were left wide open so that we could run out and climb the fire escapes. We played capture-the-flag in the auditorium, where Sun Yat-sen and Chiang Kai-shek's pictures hung at the back of the stage, the Chinese flag on their left and the American flag on their right. We climbed the teak

ceremonial chairs and made flying leaps off the stage. One flag headquarters was behind the glass door and the other on stage right. Our feet drummed on the hollow stage. During recess the teachers locked themselves up in their office with the shelves of books, copybooks, inks from China. They drank tea and warmed their hands at a stove. There was no play supervision. At recess we had the school to ourselves, and also we could roam as far as we could go—downtown, Chinatown stores, home—as long as we returned before the bell rang.

At exactly 7:30 the teacher again picked up the brass bell that sat on his desk and swung it over our heads, while we charged down the stairs, our cheering magnified in the stairwell. Nobody had to line up.

A CALIFORNIA CHRISTMAS

BY JOAQUIN MILLER

Behold where Beauty walks with Peace!
Behold where Plenty pours her horn
Of fruits, of flowers, fat increase,
As generous as light of morn.

Green Shasta, San Diego, seas
Of bloom and green between them rolled.
Great herds in grasses to their knees,
And green earth garmented in gold.

White peaks that prop the sapphire blue
Look down on Edens, such as when
That fair first spot perfection knew,
And God walked perfect earth with men.

I say God's kingdom is at hand
Right here, if we but lift our eyes;
I say there lies no line or land
Between this land and Paradise.

Nature has no mercy at all. Nature says, "I'm going to snow. If you have on a bikini and no snowshoes, that's tough. I am going to snow anyway.

—Maya Angelou

Fire-Roasted Artichokes

4 large, fresh
artichokes

Juice from
2 lemons

1 teaspoon oregano

2 tablespoons
olive oil

Salt and pepper
to taste

ARTICHOKES WERE FIRST BROUGHT TO CALIFORNIA BY THE SPANIARDS AND SUCCESSFULLY CULTIVATED IN THE MONTEREY AREA. TODAY, NEARLY 100% OF AMERICA'S ARTICHOKES ARE GROWN IN THE GOLDEN STATE, AND CASTROVILLE GROWS SO MANY THAT THEY CELEBRATE THE VEGETABLE WITH AN ARTICHOKE FESTIVAL EVERY YEAR. THIS RECIPE DRESSES THE ARTICHOKES MINIMALLY SO THAT THEIR NATURAL FLAVORS ARE SHOWCASED. DIP THE LEAVES IN A TOUCH OF AIOLI, OR ENJOY THEM DRENCHED IN THE ROASTED-TOMATO VINAIGRETTE FOR TWO DISTINCTIVE TASTE TREATS.

1. To prepare the artichokes for roasting, first cut and trim the outer leaves, removing any tough or old leaves.

2. Add lemon juice and oregano to a large pot of boiling salted water. Reduce heat to medium-low and simmer for 25 to 30 minutes. Remove from pot and allow to cool.

3. While artichokes are cooling, prepare briquettes in a BBQ Grill (gas grills are fine as well).

4. Once coals are hot and glowing, slice artichokes in half. Toss with olive oil, salt, and pepper.

5. Place, cut-side down on the grill for 5-7 minutes. You do not need to cook them much longer; you just want them to slightly char and pick up a smoky flavor. Serve with Aioli or Roasted Tomato Vinaigrette (recipes follow).

SERVES 4

ROASTED-TOMATO VINAIGRETTE:

2 large tomatoes

¹⁄₂ cup balsamic vinegar

¹⁄₂ cup olive oil

1 tablespoon brown sugar

1 tablespoon fresh chopped basil

1 clove garlic, minced

A pinch red chili flakes

Salt and pepper to taste

AIOLI:

2 cloves garlic, minced almost into a mash

1 teaspoon salt

2 large egg yolks

6 tablespoons high-quality extra-virgin olive oil

ROASTED-TOMATO VINAIGRETTE:

1. While artichokes are grilling, place tomatoes on the grill as well.

2. Once skins have blackened and charred, remove and place in a food processor, or chop by hand.

3. Add the rest of the ingredients. In a small pan, heat vinaigrette slightly and pour over artichokes.

AIOLI:

1. In a food processor or blender, combine garlic, salt, and egg yolks.

2. With the motor running, add oil. Once the right consistency is reached, add seasoning, and refrigerate until ready to use.

SALAD DAYS

California grows about 70% of all asparagus in the U.S., producing over 50,000 pounds a year. The word asparagus comes from the Greek word for "shoot" or "sprout." A wonderful source of fiber, folate, vitamin C, niacin, and thiamine, asparagus is just 45 calories a cup!

Most of California's exports of its lettuce, table grapes, and processed tomatoes are sent to our neighbor to the north, Canada.

Almond orchards produce one of the Golden State's top-20 commodities—and provide a natural habitat for wildlife such as deer, pheasant, and quail.

California's lumber industry produces nearly 2 billion board feet of commercial lumber per year— enough to build 132,000 homes!

America's first seedless oranges came from Brazil and were planted in California in 1871.

"Baby-cut" carrots aren't actually baby carrots. They're full-size ones peeled and polished down to a smaller proportion. And there's nothing tiny about their current popularity: About 25 percent of California's fresh carrot crop gets turned into "babies."

Ninety-five percent of California's raisins are made from Thompson's grapes. The sweet, thin-skinned seedless variety was developed by Scottish immigrant William Thompson in 1876.

❈ ❈ ❈

Today, Americans eat about 30 pounds of lettuce a year. That's great news for the farmers of Monterey County, who produce more than half of California's lettuce crop. They've even nicknamed their county the "Salad Bowl of the World!"

❈ ❈ ❈

Ninety-five percent of domestic apricots come from California's San Joaquin Valley, but these ancient fruits made a long journey to get there. First grown in China, they traveled across the Persian Empire to Spain, and were brought to the New World by Spanish missionaries in the 1700s.

❈ ❈ ❈

Twenty-five percent of America's cherry crop grows in the Central Valley. Each cherry tree produces fruit for about 25 years, and the average tree has 7,000 cherries a year, enough for about 28 pies per tree, per year!

❈ ❈ ❈

One hundred percent of the nation's canned peaches, fruit cocktail, and black ripe olives are grown, processed, packed, and shipped in California. That adds up to over 500,000 tons of peaches and 120,000 tons of olives a year.

❈ ❈ ❈

All commercially grown domestic artichokes are grown in California— with 75% of those coming from Castroville, the "Artichoke Capital of the World"—yet this edible thistle has only been cultivated there since the early 20th century. Castroville celebrates the harvest by crowning an Artichoke Queen each year, the very first of whom went on to become a famous movie star... none other than Marilyn Monroe!

❈ ❈ ❈

That's a lot of guacamole! California is the largest producer of avocados in America, and Fallbrook, California is known as (you guessed it!) the Avocado Capital of the World. A mature tree can yield as many as 400 avocados a year.

STING   WINE

N

ZONE

Reno

Virginia
City

CARSON
CITY

CASTLE PEAK

A

L

I

F

O

R

N

I

A

MT. HOUGH

MT. LYELL

MT. LANE

MT. WHITNEY

Bakersfield

Los Angeles

MT. SAN BERNARDINO

Colorado R.

San Bernardino

Wilmington

THE GOLDEN GATE

AREA 158,360 SQ. MILES

POPULATION 864,694

The Recall—The recall of Governor Gray Davis in 2003 captivated not only Californians, but the entire nation. With 135 candidates vying for the state's top job, this wildly disparate group included a former child actor, a pornographer, a lieutenant governor, and an action-film star. Though the recall had never been used to remove someone from the governorship, this legislation had been implemented in 1910 to increase voters' rights and curtail the power of special interest groups. At that time, Southern Pacific Railroad controlled transportation and the media, and the recall was a way of overturning legislation by bringing issues straight to the voters. Though rarely used before (not a single government official was recalled before 1995), the people of California turned to the recall when they felt that the governor had mismanaged the state's finances and mishandled the energy crisis. Some companies investing in California's deregulating energy

HARD TIMES: POLITICAL AND SOCIAL UNREST

markets used unscrupulous accounting practices which fueled climbing energy prices, leading to electricity shortages, rolling blackouts and financial troubles for the state. When all was said and done, Gray Davis was ousted and replaced by "The Governator"—Arnold Schwarzenegger. History will judge whether the recall is a dangerous weapon used to undermine government leaders, or a necessary democratic tool to keep California's politicians in check.

Watts and L.A. Riots—In times of depressed economic conditions and in the face of racial oppression, one event can set off a firestorm of reaction that can destroy nearly everything in its path. Such was the case in the town of Watts on August 11, 1965, where Marquette Frye, an African-American man, was pulled over under suspicion of driving drunk by a white LAPD officer. As the police questioned Frye and his brother, a crowd formed and grew angry when the brothers were arrested (with their motherwho had arrived on the scene). After police left, tempers flared and rioting began. The six days of violence left 34 people dead, 1,100 injured, and over $100 million in damage. A gubernatorial commission identified high unemployment, substandard schools, and impoverished living conditions as contributing factors to the riots, but the state made little effort to address these issues or repair the community.

Nearly 30 years later, the nation would again find itself suffering from recession, one that hit the South Central neighborhood of L.A. particularly hard. When a bystander with a videotape recorder captured the police beating of an African-American named Rodney King, the community and the nation were outraged. In 1992, when the four cops involved were acquitted of using excessive force, violent riots erupted that required the California National Guard and thousands of soldiers from the Army and Marines to quell the chaos. In the end, more than 50 people were killed, 600 fires set, 10,000 people arrested, and nearly $1 billion in damages done.

The AIDS Crisis in San Francisco—In the early eighties, a dangerous phenomenon appeared in the gay community of San Francisco. A rare cancer, known as Kaposi's sarcoma, and an opportunistic lung infection Pneumocystis carinii pneumonia (PCP) were showing up in gay men, many of whom sickened and died in the months following diagnosis. While the Center for Disease Control struggled to identify the causes of this new killer, fear spread about the so-called "gay cancer," later renamed AIDS. As bathhouses were closed in an effort to contain the disease, the San Francisco gay community came together to help educate the public about AIDS and care for the sick who were being shunned by the public at large. AIDS Awareness spread throughout the country as the disease began to spread to all walks of life. San Francisco became the epicenter of treatment and support for those affected, and spawned projects such as the AIDS Quilt, which contains panels commemorating the lives of those lost to AIDS.

Harvey Milk—The first openly gay elected official in any large city in America, Supervisor Milk was gunned down at City Hall along with Mayor George Moscone in 1978. Extremely popular in the gay community of San Francisco, Milk was often referred to as the "Mayor of Castro Street." His killer, Dan White, had resigned from his city supervisor role when a gay rights bill he opposed was enacted. He was convicted of manslaughter on the grounds of diminished capacity, and given the light sentence of seven years in jail. Lawyers claimed that White's consumption of junk food was uncharacteristic of the normally health-conscious man and indicative of depression, which became widely referred to as the "Twinkie" defense. The gay community of San Francisco was outraged by the sentence and the White Night riots erupted—leaving more than160 hospitalized. Harvey Milk is widely regarded as a martyr for the gay rights movement. The Academy award-winning film *The Times of Harvey Milk* commemorates his life and struggle for equal rights.

Black Panthers—During the turbulent sixties, an era where nonviolent protests for civil rights issues were at the forefront of the nation's consciousness, Huey Newton and Bobby Seale had a different idea of how to obtain equal standing as black citizens. In 1966, in Oakland, they formed the Black Panther Party for Self-Defense (later known simply as the Black Panthers Party) to protect African-Americans from police brutality. They eventually morphed into a socialist group which espoused the creation of economic, political, and social equality for all blacks. Because they believed in the right to defend themselves by any means necessary, they were constantly at odds with non-violent civil rights groups, the police, and FBI.

In 1967, Newton was sent to prison on a manslaughter conviction after a shoot-out with police in Oakland, but was released in 1971 after his conviction was overturned. He later attempted to steer the group away from violent confrontation and toward the creation of community programs. Most notably, the Black Panthers began programs that offered free breakfasts to children before school, free medical clinics, and free clothing and food for those in need. By the 1980s the party had effectively disbanded.

Free Speech Movement at Berkeley—In the fall of 1964, many students returned to the campus of the University of California at Berkeley after spending the summer participating in the civil rights marches in the South, and wanted to share their political views. The school administration took issue with the students and banned them from using school grounds to promote political causes, sign students up for groups, or collect funds for student causes. One student set up a table in protest of the ban, and was arrested, but students surrounded the police car and staged a sit-in until charges were dropped. The issue did not die there, however. An even larger protest in December of 1964 virtually shut down the campus when more than 800 students were arrested for staging a massive sit-in in Sproul Hall, the administration building. By January of 1965, the administration backed down and relaxed the rules for political activity on campus. To this day, Sproul Plaza is a lightening rod for protests and marches involving free speech.

Zoot-Suit Riots—In the early 1940s, L.A. became a hotbed of ethnic tensions. Japanese-Americans had been taken to internment camps, and Latinos were being harassed by military soldiers because of their style of dress. The "zoot suit"—a broad-shouldered long coat, with peg-leg, high-waisted trousers, and wide-brim hats—was a popular fashion statement with Latino men. The military resented them for not being soldiers (though a disproportionately high number of Latinos *were* serving in the military), and the press stirred fears of a "Mexican crime wave." Any Latino in a zoot suit was immediately identified as a gangster.

On the night of June 3, 1943, a number of sailors said they had been mugged by zoot suiters, causing an angry military mob to invade East Los Angeles, beating and stripping any young Latino they could find. Since police did little to stop the mob, the soldiers were emboldened and continued their assault on the barrio for three more nights. Finally on June 7th, the military took action and barred the servicemen from Los Angeles, but the press heralded the soldiers for fighting the "Mexican crime wave." Although mostly victims, more than 500 Latinos were jailed for vagrancy and rioting, and the military claimed self-defense. The country condemned the riots, and First Lady Eleanor Roosevelt was especially vocal, calling it a racial protest and saying, "We do not always face these problems as we should." The *Los Angeles Times* accused her of being a communist.

THE COPS AND ROBBERS GAME

BY *TOM WOLFE*

A very carnival! and it wasn't politics, what he said, just a prank, because the political thing, the whole New Left, is all of a sudden like *over* on the hip circuit around San Francisco, even at Berkeley, the very citadel of the Student Revolution and all. Some kid who could always be counted on to demonstrate for the grape workers or even do dangerous things like work for CORE in Mississippi turns up one day— and immediately everybody knows he has become a head. His hair has the long jesuschrist look. He is wearing the costume clothes. But most of all, he now has a very tolerant and therefore withering attitude toward all those who are still struggling in the old activist political ways for civil rights, against Vietnam, against poverty, for the free peoples. He sees them as still trapped in the old "political games," unwittingly supporting the oppressors by playing their kind of game and using their kind of tactics, while he, with the help of psychedelic chemicals, is exploring the infinite regions of human consciousness...Paul Hawken here in The Embassy—in 1965 he was an outstanding activist, sweat shirts and blue jeans and toggle coats, when on the March from Selma, worked as a photographer for CORE in Mississippi, risked his life to take pictures of Negro working conditions, and so on. Now he's got on a great Hussar's coat with gold frogging. His hair is all over his forehead and coming around his neck in terrific black Mykonos curls.

Split Pea Soup

1 tablespoon olive oil

2 medium onions, diced

4 cloves garlic, chopped

1 ham bone

¼ pound bacon, diced

20 large shrimp, peeled and deveined

1 cup celery leaves and stalks, chopped

2 cups split peas, dried

10 cups chicken stock or water

Salt and pepper to taste

Pea Soup Andersen's of Buellton, California has built its fortunes on this ubiquitous comfort food. With a campy billboard featuring the cartoon chefs Hap-Pea and Pea-Wee trying to split a pea with a hammer and chisel and stirring a pot of soup, Andersen's has become a California landmark. The popularity of pea soup in the '20s helped launch this restaurant founded by Anton and Julliette Andersen in 1927. Our rendition of this California favorite will bring you back to your childhood spot in a cozy booth at Andersen's.

1. In a large stockpot, heat olive oil over medium-high heat.

2. Add onions, garlic, ham bone, and bacon, cooking until the onions are tender.

3. Add carrots, celery, split peas, and stock or water.

4. Bring to a boil and then simmer, uncovered for 1 ½ hours, stirring occasionally and skimming off any foam that accumulates.

5. Season with salt and pepper, and serve.

Serves 8

MAIN STREET, USA, beckoned whenever my mother felt homesick. She and my sisters and I would climb into the car, and Dad would steer east out of Lakewood, "Tomorrow's City Today." He almost always took surface streets: My mom was frightened by freeways.

DISNEYLAND

BY RICHARD STAYTON

When my dad caught the great California fever of 1960, he packed our family into a Nash Rambler and drove west to seek his fortune. Here dad thrived in his new job at North American Aviation, but Mom, who had never roamed far from her Indiana town of 5,000, missed her mother, her relatives, the soda fountain, the "picture show," the Methodist Church, and just sitting quietly on the front porch at sunset, listening to crickets and watching the fireflies. Above all, my mother missed the small-town Saturday night ritual of Main Street, of strolling the sidewalk without a destination, waving to friends and neighbors.

Dad kept trying to cure her of the need to return to the "promised land," as he came to call southern Indiana, by "showing us the sights" of Southern California. We cruised Hollywood Boulevard and the Miracle Mile, walked along Olvera Street, and strolled the beaches of Long Beach. We saw Dodgers outfielder

Wally Moon pop a home run over the temporary fence of the Coliseum. Yet only one place made my mother truly happy.

For us, Disneyland truly was the "Happiest Place on Earth." The moment we stepped through the gates onto Main Street, we were home. First we'd sit on the benches in the park by City Hall, absorbing the magic. Under the Disney trees my parents grew talkative—a rare event for those shy Midwesterners. Dad would talk about the vintage Model A, which had been his first car, as a Disney replica tooted by. Mom remembered cutting her fur coat into pieces to make me a coonskin cap during the Davy Crockett craze, when every kid longed to be "King of the Wild Frontier." Then we'd separate according to lands, agreeing to meet later for dinner on Main Street. Disneyland was the only place in the perplexing colossus of Southern California where our parents allowed us to roam without supervision as we always had done back home. Uncle Walt, an old Midwesterner too, had been with us in Indiana through his Sunday night TV show. My parents could rest easy, knowing we were cradled in his protective embrace.

Churros

Vegetable oil

1 cup water

¹⁄₂ cup butter

¹⁄₄ teaspoon salt

1 lemon, zested

1 cup all-purpose flour

3 eggs, lightly beaten

¹⁄₂ cup sugar

1 tablespoon ground cinnamon

CHOCOLATE DIPPING SAUCE

2 cups milk

1 tablespoon cornstarch

4 tablespoons sugar

4 ounces dark chocolate, chopped

THIS CRISPY PASTRY WAS INVENTED BY SHEPHERDS IN SPAIN CENTURIES AGO, WHO MADE FRIED BREAD SWEETENED WITH SUGAR. EVENTUALLY THE TREAT WAS FORMED INTO A STAR SHAPE, AND NAMED AFTER THE CHURRO SHEEP WHOSE HORNS THE PASTRY RESEMBLED. WHEN THE SPANISH CONQUISTADORS CAME TO THE NEW WORLD, THEY BROUGHT CHURROS WITH THEM AND SPREAD THEIR POPULARITY THROUGHOUT MEXICO AND CALIFORNIA. ENJOY THIS SIMPLE RECIPE IN THE TRADITIONAL WAY, OR WITH A LUSCIOUS CHOCOLATE DIPPING SAUCE.

1. Prepare to fry the churros by heating oil in a large heavy-bottomed frying pan (or deep fat fryer) to 350°F.

2. Heat water, butter, salt, and lemon zest to a rolling boil in a large saucepan.

3. Over low heat, stir in flour until mixture forms a ball, about 1 minute. Remove from heat.

4. Beat in eggs. Continue beating until smooth.

5. In a large, shallow container, mix sugar and cinnamon.

6. Spoon churro batter into a cake decorator's tube or bag fitted with a large star tip. Using equal pressure, carefully squeeze 4-inch strips of dough into the hot oil.

7. Fry 3 or 4 strips at a time until golden brown, turning as needed to maintain even cooking and color.

8. Drain on paper towels slightly before rolling in cinnamon sugar. Serve immediately.

9. If you'd like to spice up your churros, try adding this delicious chocolate dipping sauce. It's rich and indulgent...and oh so good!

CHOCOLATE DIPPING SAUCE

1. In a small saucepan, heat milk over medium-high heat, stirring occasionally. (You do not want to boil the milk, just raise the temperature to a simmer.)

2. Reduce heat to low.

3. Place 1 cup of warmed milk in a small bowl. Add cornstarch and sugar, stirring until they dissolve.

4. Add chopped chocolate to remaining milk in saucepan and whisk until smooth.

5. Add milk-cornstarch mixture to the chocolate and whisk until smooth and thick, about 5 minutes. Serve warm alongside churros.

SERVES 4

CALIFORNIA'S DISTINCTIVE CHARACTER owes much to the rich culture that flows northward from Mexico and Latin America, commonly known as "South of the Border." For a taste of this influence, you

SOUTH-OF-THE-BORDER INFLUENCES

need only travel just south of San Diego to Tijuana, a city of over one million residents in northwestern Mexico. Tijuana is famous for its bullfighting arenas, gorgeous beaches, historical sites, lively discos, and bustling shopping centers. Every year, more than 64 million people cross between California and Tijuana, making that stretch of land the most-crossed international border in the world. Film and music stars, such as Rita Hayworth, Dolores del Rio, and Santana, were discovered in Tijuana, where, as legend has it, the margarita was invented as a non-alcoholic drink for Hayworth (born Margarita-Margarita Carmen Cansino) when she was a teenage cabaret performer. Also, the ubiquitous Caesar salad was first concocted at Caesar's Palace restaurant on Tijuana's *Avenida Revolucion*, one of the world's most-shopped streets.

Mexican and Latin American cooking heavily flavors California's eclectic cuisine. Many southern Californians favor tacos, enchiladas, and "Tex-Mex" (Texan-Mexican) dishes. And though San Franciscans and their more-northern neighbors may specialize in Asian and Italian styles of cooking, many of the ingredients they use are of Spanish origin. This Californian mixing of ethnic styles is often called fusion cuisine. Californians have also perfected and popularized the *wrap*—that is, a tortilla wrapped around meat, fish, or vegetables—and use salsas in all type of dips, spreads, and marinades. To wash it down, a Californian might make a tasty pitcher of Mexican sangria, mixing red wine, orange juice, lime juice, sugar, and adding apple slices.

South-of-the-border characteristics also pervade Californian architecture. Southern California teems with buildings made of white-stucco walls and red-tiled roofs, some of which feature curved gables, arched windows, and a bell tower or balcony. Plainer structures exemplify the *Mission Revival* style, while newer, more ornate buildings represent the *Spanish Colonial* style. In actuality, the first Spanish-speaking Californios lived in one-story, tarred-roofed adobe houses (fashioned from clay mixed with hay); the original missions were also adobe. But the modern, more Mediterranean-based "mission" style became popular in the late 1800s as architects re-envisioned the older designs and Californians expressed sentimental longings for romanticized versions of their own history.

Though Californians overwhelmingly voted for Proposition 227 in 1998 (an initiative that basically eliminated bilingual education in public schools), Spanish words and phrases from south of the border increasingly find their way into Californian and national parlance. Spanish-speaking neighborhoods in California are customarily referred to as *barrios*; in the Hollywood mega-hit *Terminator 2: Judgment*

Day (1991), California's current Governor Arnold Schwarzenegger famously muttered "*Hasta la vista*, baby;" and the former Secretary of State Madeline Albright characterized the 1996 Cuban downing of two U.S. civilian planes as cowardice, "no *cojones*." By 2000, Los Angeles' highest-rated TV and radio stations (such as the L.A.—based Univision network which is part-owned by Televisa, Mexico's largest broadcasting network) were Spanish-language broadcasters.

Latin American telenovelas—topical daily soap operas that usually end after 180 to 200 episodes—are very popular among Californian Spanish-speaking viewers and make up a large share of primetime programming on Spanish-language stations. Before becoming a star in Hollywood, Salma Hayek made a name for herself in Mexico with her celebrated 1990's soap opera roles. Thalia, a singing and acting sensation whose global star is on the rise, also began her career as a Mexican telenovela star. Erik Estrada (originally of the TV show *CHiP's*) and Ricky Martin (originally of boy band *Menudo*) found second careers crossing over to the beloved Mexican soaps. Both men eventually used their Mexican popularity to propel them back to American stardom. Estrada took a role in the U.S. soap *The Bold and the Beautiful*, and Martin launched a solo pop career.

As California welcomes new immigrants from our neighbors to the south, its culture continues to absorb their many influences. Their impact is seen, smelled, tasted, heard, and felt in the distinctive food, architecture, language, and entertainment of modern-day California.

SURF'S UP

Modern surfing hails from the Hawaiian practice of *he'e nalu*, or "wave sliding." Referred to as "the sport of Kings," it was mainly practiced by affluent members of ancient Hawaiian society. Priests called Kahunas would pray for excellent surfing conditions.

When white settlers (*haole*) brought western religion to the Sandwich Islands, the spiritual aspects of surfing were lost. Forced to adapt, surfing fell out of favor with the natives in the late 18th century and was not popular again until the early 20th century.

George Freeth, a native Hawaiian of Irish descent, introduced surfing to California in 1907. He demonstrated the sport at Redondo Beach to publicize the Redondo-Los Angeles railroad. Freeth stayed on to become California's first lifeguard and became known as "the Father of American Surfing."

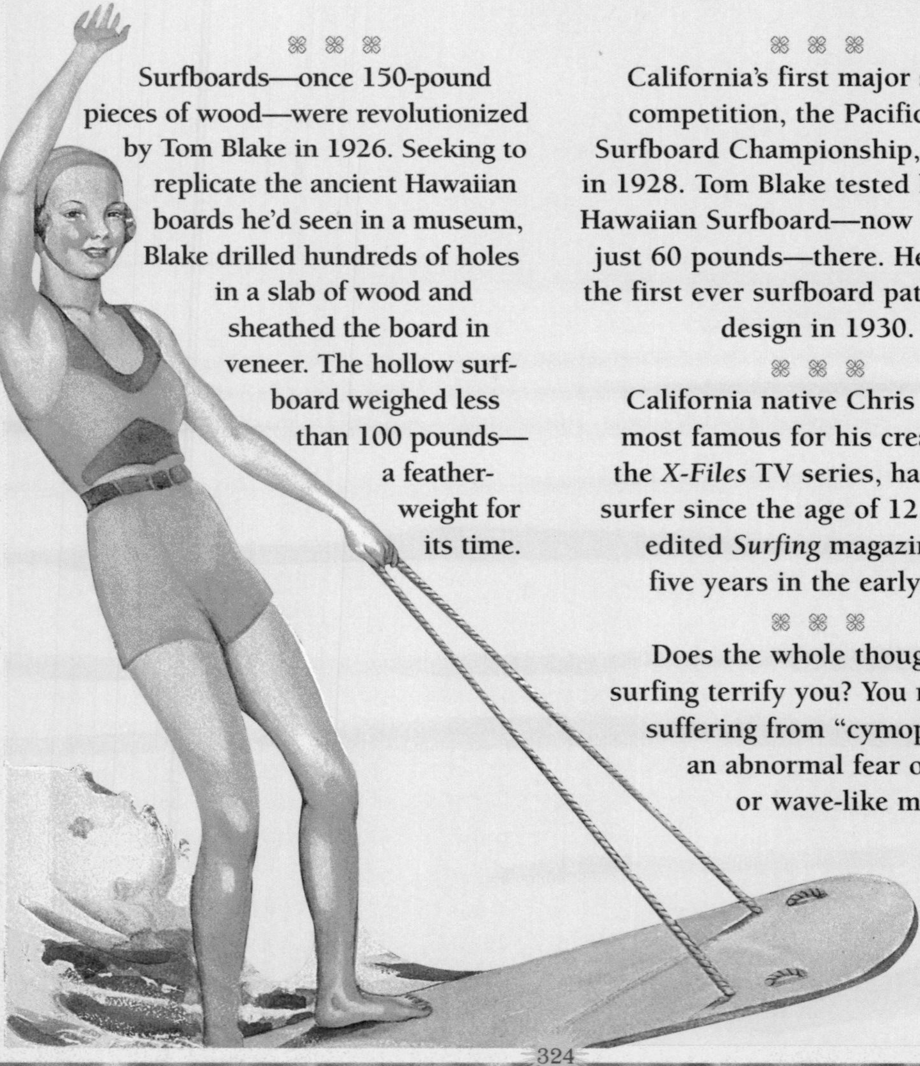

❈ ❈ ❈

Surfboards—once 150-pound pieces of wood—were revolutionized by Tom Blake in 1926. Seeking to replicate the ancient Hawaiian boards he'd seen in a museum, Blake drilled hundreds of holes in a slab of wood and sheathed the board in veneer. The hollow surfboard weighed less than 100 pounds— a featherweight for its time.

❈ ❈ ❈

California's first major surfing competition, the Pacific Coast Surfboard Championship, was held in 1928. Tom Blake tested his Hallow Hawaiian Surfboard—now reduced to just 60 pounds—there. He received the first ever surfboard patent for his design in 1930.

❈ ❈ ❈

California native Chris Carter, most famous for his creation of the *X-Files* TV series, has been a surfer since the age of 12. He even edited *Surfing* magazine for five years in the early '80s.

❈ ❈ ❈

Does the whole thought of surfing terrify you? You might be suffering from "cymophobia," an abnormal fear of waves or wave-like motions.

Surfing experienced its golden age
in California during the '50s and '60s,
as Hollywood romanticized surf
culture in movies like *Gidget*
and Americans began to see it as a
pastime every one could enjoy.

Dale Velzy and Hap Jacobs also helped
bring surfing to the masses by opening
the first commercial surfboard
production in 1953, popularizing
their lighter balsa-wood boards.

In the 1920s, surfboards averaged
75-150 pounds, with some of the
16-foot, plank-style boards (inspired
by ancient Hawaiian *olo* solid-wood
models) weighing as much as
200 pounds. Today's surfboards
can weigh as little as five pounds!

All the leaves are brown,
And the sky is grey.
I've been for a walk
on a winter's day.

I'd be safe and warm,
if I was in L.A.
California dreamin'
On such a winter's day.

Stopped into a church,
I passed along the way.
Oh, I got down on my knees,
And I pretend to pray.
You know the preacher likes
    the cold,

He knows I'm gonna stay.
California dreamin'
On such a winter's day.

All the leaves are brown,
And the sky is grey
I've been for a walk
on a winter's day.

If I didn't tell her
I could leave today.
California dreamin'
On such a winter's day.

CALIFORNIA
DREAMIN'

BY JOHN PHILLIPS

326

NESTLED IN THE SOUTHERN San Francisco Bay area, Silicon Valley is the nickname for a roughly 30- by 10-mile stretch that extends from Palo Alto, southeast through communities such as Sunnyvale and Cupertino, and on down to San Jose. In 1971, journalist Don Hoefler first coined the name to describe the current home of many high-tech computer-based industries. ("Silicon" is the substance used to make semiconductors for computers.)

It all began in the 1930s, when a Stanford University engineering professor worried about eastward brain drain decided to entice graduates to stay in California by providing funds and equipment. Two recruits formed Hewlett-Packard (HP)—a company that achieved innovation through

SILICON VALLEY

corporate decentralization, the free-flow of information, continuing education, and employee autonomy and satisfaction—and originated Silicon Valley's singular work and management style. Stanford also began strategically leasing land to technical companies. In 1954, HP rented space, and soon General Electric, Eastman Kodak, and other companies joined them. The seeds of Silicon Valley were sown.

The 1950s witnessed the birth of the transistor, an apparatus that replaced larger, less- efficient vacuum tubes by using solid semiconducting material to magnify electronic images. When major defense contractor Lockheed relocated to Sunnyvale in 1956, the Valley's semiconductor industry got a crucial boost. Companies were also attracted to Silicon Valley because of its pleasant climate, abundance of industrial space, inexpensive housing, and high concentration of well-trained workers. By the early 1970s, the Valley was brimming with firms making semiconductors and using them to build computers. Intel's integrated circuit semiconductor "chips" and CPU 8088s became the industry standards. But by the mid-1980s, Japanese semiconductor manufacturers were using better production processes coupled with good supplier and customer relations to dominate the industry.

Just in time, new life came to Silicon Valley in the form of personal computers. Apple's machine took off in 1977, and before long IBM and HP entered the fray. In the early 1980s, the PC revolution spawned many other products and industries, such as printers, disk drives, video games, and computer-aided design. After Apple's successful $1.3 billion initial public offering (IPO) in 1980, venture capital became readily available to Valley entrepreneurs. Silicon Valley's next technological wave involved the Internet. In 1981, a new company called Sun Microsystems began designing and licensing network file sharing software, and in 1984 Cisco Systems developed technology to integrate many local networks into one. When Netscape launched the first mass-marketed Internet browser in the early '90s, the Internet caught fire.

By the late '90s, Silicon Valley was known around the world for its techno-logical innovations, dynamic companies, and dot-com millionaires. It was a crazy place to work. Everyone seemed to be toying with new ideas, developing business plans, raising venture capital, and getting rich from IPOs and stock options. Both 1999 and 2000 saw more than 250 venture capital-backed tech IPOs. But by 2001, due to many factors including rising interest rates, the over-buying of computer equipment in preparation for Y2K, and flawed dot-com models, the bubble had burst. In 2002, the Valley lost 10 percent of its jobs; there were only 19 IPOs.

Many say Silicon Valley's next wave of growth will probably combine biotechnology, nanotechnology, and information-based technology. But regional industries must find new ways of staying competitive. Rival tech centers in China, India, and Taiwan, offer equally educated yet cheaper labor; the technology downturn is discouraging young Americans from studying computer science; post 9/11 visa restrictions make it harder for foreign students to attend U.S. universities; and local firms often complain of the high cost of living and doing business in the area. Silicon Valley is no longer an international icon. Nevertheless, companies such as eBay, Oracle, and Yahoo! continue to grow, and the Valley forges on.

FLYING ABOVE CALIFORNIA

BY THOM GUNN

Spread beneath me it lies—lean upland
sinewed and tawny in the sun, and

valley cool with mustard, or sweet with
loquat. I repeat under my breath

names of places I have not been to:
Crescent City, San Bernardino

—Mediterranean and Northern names.
Such richness can make you drunk. Sometimes

on fogless days by the Pacific,
there is a cold hard light without break

that reveals merely what is—no more
and no less. That limiting candor,

that accuracy of the beaches,
is part of the ultimate richness.

THE RAILROAD DIDN'T BELIEVE in lengthy formal training. They offered a two-week class which covered the book of rules, a three-hundred-page document with a dual purpose—to keep trains from running into one another and to prevent any situation in which the company might get sued. Rules of the road which you had to learn were mixed in with rules which you had to ignore in order to get the work done. But you had to know that you were ignoring a rule so that in the winter, when company officials had time to sneak around testing, you could work by the book.

BOOMER

BY LINDA NIEMANN

The rulebook was also in a continuous state of revision. Revisions appeared in the timetable which you carried with you at all times. Further revisions appeared in regular timetable bulletins which were posted at work. Soon your rulebook resembled a scrapbook, with paragraphs crossed out, pages pasted in, and notes on changes which were then crossed out and changed weeks later. It drove you crazy. You always had to be on the lookout for a company official hiding in the bushes while you did your work. This individual would pop out and ask you questions about the latest rule revisions. A notation of failure would then appear in your personal file. These notations were referred to as "Brownies," named after the official who devised the railroad demerit system. As trainmen were fond of pointing out, however, there was no merit system to go with it.

Out of seventeen student brakemen three of us were women. This was a large percentage, comparatively. The first women had been hired two years before, and they were around to give us advice. The point was to get through the class, ignore the sexist remarks and the scare tactics, and get over the probationary period known as the "derail." Then you were in the union and a railroader for life. Getting over the derail took sixty days, and if either the crews you worked with or the company officers had a complaint, you were out. At the end of two weeks of classroom instruction, you bought a railroad watch, they gave you switch keys and a two-dollar lantern, and you marked up as extra board brakemen. It was going to be sink or swim in this business. We drew numbers to determine our seniority dates—the most important factor in our careers. One or two numbers could mean that you worked or didn't.

On the last day of class, they took us down to the freightyard to grapple with the equipment. We practiced getting on and off moving cars, climbing the ladders and cranking down the handbrakes, lacing up the airhoses and cutting in the air, changing the

eighty-five-pound knuckles that joined the cars together, and hand and lantern signals. These signals were the way members of the crew talked to each other, and they were an art form. An old head could practically order an anchovy pizza from a half mile away. You would see lights, arcs and circles, stabs of light. It would repeat. You would stand there confused. Finally you would walk down the track and find the foreman in a deep state of disgust.

"I told you to hand three cars, let two go to the runaround, one to the main, go through the crossovers, and line behind. Now can't you read a signal, dummy?"

The day after our practice session, I got into my car and tried to roll the window down. My arms didn't work. This was my first moment of doubt about being able to do the job. It was hard to get the upper-body strength required to hang on and ride for long distances on the side of cars. Terror at falling beneath the wheels was a big motivator, however. Terror and ridicule. There was a lot of both during the probationary period and the student trips. On student trips we tagged along with a regular crew and tried to learn something. To me, what we were doing made no sense whatsoever. Just getting used to the equipment had me so disoriented that I had no idea where we had gone or how the crew did anything. One of the crew suggested to me that I go to a toy store and look at the model trains, to see how switches work. They say, though, that whatever you start out doing rail-roading, it gets imprinted, and that's what you are most comfortable doing from then on. I couldn't have picked a better place to break in than Watsonville Junction. It was old-time, local-freight, full-crew switching. Kicking cars and passing signs. The basic stuff that you have to learn at first or you never get no matter how long you're out here.

The small switching yard at Watsonville classified all the perishable freight from the Salinas Valley and Hollister-Gilroy—the "salad bowl" of America. A break in the coastal range at Salinas allowed the fog to pour into the valley, cooling it, and allowing cool weather crops like artichokes, brussels sprouts, and lettuce to grow. Strawberry fields and apple orchards skirted the low hillsides. There were cool fresh days in midsummer. The packing houses and canneries were running around the clock, with rows of mostly women working the graveyard assembly lines. Clusters of yellow school buses bordered the fields, and farmworkers moved slowly through the orderly rows, bundled up against the fog and pesticides.

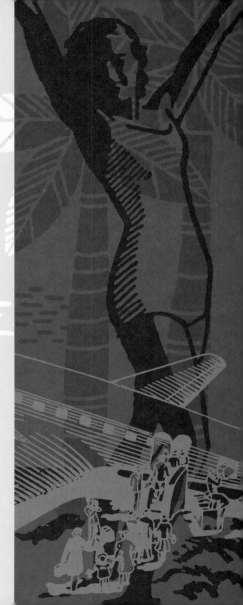

From LEAVES OF GRASS

BY WALT WHITMAN

Facing west from California's shores,
Inquiring, tireless, seeking what is yet unfound,
I, a child, very old, over waves, towards the house of
     maternity, the land of
     migrations, look afar,
Look off the shores of my Western sea, the circle
     almost circled;
For starting westward from Hindustan, from the
     vales of Kashmere,
From Asia, from the north, from the God, the sage,
     and the hero,
From the south, from the flowery peninsulas and the
     spice islands,
Long having wander'd since, round the earth having
     wander'd,
Now I face home again, very pleas'd and joyous,
(But where is what I started for so long ago?
And why is it unfound?)

FROM ALL THE LITTLE LIVE THINGS
BY WALLACE STEGNER

December 12, the calendar tells me. Two months since the Catlin cottage went dark.

All through the past weeks the storms have come spinning in off the Pacific, and the microclimates of the foothills have been swept together and obliterated in rain, like petty differences of opinion in a crisis. Each new storm arrives with a pounce, and our house anchored on its hilltop shakes to the padded blows of the wind, and the trees heave and creak, and our terrace is littered with twigs and berries. We fear for our windows pounded and streaming, and look out across the terrace to see horizontal bursts of rain combing the treetops below us, blurring the ugliness of Weld's interrupted excavations across the gully.

Even the lichened oak outside my study window, with limbs larger around than my body, is uneasy in the wind. There is a stiff arthritic movement in it as if the 6600 volts of turmoil tearing through its upper branches have been stepped down, here in the underleaf cave, to a housebroken 110. The soggy duff on the ground is constantly kicked around by juncos and Oregon towhees and golden-crowned sparrows, and the presence of these birds, which we watch with pleasure and for

which I have built a feeding tray out of Catarrh's reach, communicates a certain uneasiness to our minds, for they ought to mean spring and actually mean winter, and the winter they mean is so confused with spring that one used to the standard seasons is bewildered.

Much of what the eye sees is Novemberish. The apricot orchards are bare, and blown downwind and plastered against walls and fences are those leaves of pistachio, liquidambar, and Japanese maple that gave us a brief New England color. Like other immigrants, we brought the familiar to an unfamiliar place, our planting impulse no different from that of pioneer women hoarding in their baggage seed of lobelia and bittersweet, or Johnny Appleseed scattering civilization along a thousand miles of frontier tracks. Call it the Law of Dispersion and Uniformity. Marian, who valued the indigenous over the exotic, was almost the only person I ever knew who didn't submit to it, and even she would sometimes take pleasure in the results.

A false autumn, then, imported but half persuasive. Now in December the earth smells Labradorean. If we had not lived through two California winter we would expect snow. And indeed we do get something wintry enough, for on clear morning we may look out our windows and see the redwood screeds of the patio wearing a pelt of frost. Sometimes the bricks are lacquered with ice, and when we drive out on early errands the lonely untracked bottoms are white, and so are the rails and post tops of Debby's corral, and so are the treads of Weld's miserable bridge, still unrepaired.

And yet under ice and frost the sand between our patio bricks has sprouted in intersecting lines of bright green moss. Within ten days of the first rain the bedraggled stubble of the hills could be parted with a toe and show tiny cotyledons of filaree and burr clover and tine spears of oat grass. All during the weeks when the year has been darkening toward its end, the green has forced itself upward through the brown, until now at close to Christmas the hills are voluptuous lawns, and the lavender branches of the delicious oaks spread against a background like April. The coyote brush, hardy and forehanded, has been blooming white since November.

Unsystematic, contradictory, unlike anything that habit and literature have led us to expect, the rainy season *is* a season, profoundly different from the summer it succeeds. It is green, not golden; wet, not dry; chilly, not warm; clear, not milky. It has real clouds, not the high fog that obscures the summer sky. It produces real sunsets, not tame quenchings of daylight. It attracts whole populations of wither birds. It smells different.

Watching the still unfamiliar changes come on, I can't help realizing that nearly our entire acquaintance with Marian was on the other cycle. The smells in the memory of sun, sage, dust, the faint dry tannic odor of sun-beaten redwood, above all of tarweed. Her light is hot and yellow or warm and brown, never the damp green of this season. She moves from high spring to summer, and stops. In the chilly, fishy smell of wet mold or the freshness of a rain-cleaned wind off the skyline there is no trace of

her. One must go back for her, and that means re-creating not only herself but the season she inhabited.

It was a season so fresh that, even remembered, it has all the feel of a beginning. That was Marian's doing. We thought of ourselves as old settlers, but settlers, but she made us newcomers again. Until the Catlins came we hardly had a social life, only a set of comfortable habits, a finicky separation from our own and all other history, and a disinclination to all acquaintance except the least demanding. In her passion to live her way into the new place, Marian pulled us after her; or rather, she set us to thinking what the Catlins must see, whom they must meet. Who would respond with the proper enthusiasm to this girl's vividness? What persons, houses, views, would excite her? Who ought to hear John, in his dry down-Maine voice, tell stories of expeditions he had been on, or expound the sonar system of porpoises, or prove that whales were once land animals by demonstrating their modified limbs and residual hair?

A Californian who is just long enough settled to be able to mispronounce Spanish names correctly is a spider, he lies in wait to initiate others into the land of his temperate exile. Not quite anything, he has to show off everything. Somewhat to our surprise, we turned out to be that kind of Californian. The Catlins, who had spent the winter in a furnished apartment downtown, with only one car and John away part of the time, had had little time to look around. They were predestined victims.